Paige

Paige

by

Jerry B. Jenkins

MOODY PRESS

CHICAGO

To Clayton Baumann

©1981 by
JERRY B. JENKINS

Library of Congress Cataloging in Publication Data

Jenkins, Jerry B
  Paige.

  I. Title
PS3560.E485P3   813'.54   80-39501
ISBN: 0-8024-4314-1 (pbk.)

4 5 6 7 Printing/LC/Year 87 86 85 84 83

Printed in the United States of America

Chapter One

The four of us who worked for him in his EH Detective Agency simply thought Earl Haymeyer was in love. It was unusual, sure—even out of character for him—but none of us fathomed how it would affect us.

Bonnie, our receptionist and secretary, had been with Earl just a few days less than I had—about a year. My fiancee, Margo Franklin, had been a special agent for about six months, following her training. And Larry Shipman, an old friend of Earl's since he had been with the United States attorney's office, had joined just a few months before.

Shipman is crazy. There's no other way to say it. He's an overgrown kid in his early thirties who never got tired of chasing police cars and fire trucks. He had helped Earl on some cases during my first few months on the job while he was a stringer for local newspapers and radio and television stations. He was also a part-time undercover man and jack-of-all-trades.

Margo and I have grown to love the Ship, especially his mock fear whenever Bonnie announces that Earl either wants him on the phone or is on his way to the office. "Now I'll be fired for sure," Larry screams, scurrying to look busy, as if he weren't the most valuable pro on the staff.

But the day Earl arrived unexpectedly at the office, and Bonnie tipped off the three of us on the intercom in the darkroom, Larry really did think he'd had it.

Earl had told us to wait for him before we tried developing the film he had shot the night before in total darkness. He explained that infrared light made it possible, and although Margo and I were skeptical, Shipman insisted he had "read something about that somewhere," as he always did when someone brought up something he knew nothing about.

Earl had left early in the morning to visit his thirteen-year-old son, Earl, Jr., who had been locked into autism since birth. Though the boy never knew Earl or his wife—who had died seven years before—Earl visited him at least once a month and generally stayed several hours to watch him play.

When Earl called Bonnie and told her he would be a little later than usual getting back, Shipman and I tried to convince each other that Earl would be just as anxious as we were to see the results of his infrared camera experiment. As usual, Margo argued for sanity. "He spent a lot of money on that camera, and he doesn't need you two rummies messing with the first roll of film he put through it."

"You don't have to be party to it if you don't want to," Shipman told her. "But I'm going to develop it and see what we've got. It's hard to believe there will be an image on the film. All he did was shoot his apartment without any light in the middle of the night. Yup. I'm going to develop the film and blame it on Philip."

I laughed, and Margo and I followed him into the darkroom.

Larry was just hanging the negatives to dry when Bonnie announced Earl. "Boss's here!" she said cheerily, knowing exactly what we were up to.

Shipman jumped and swore.

"She's kidding," I said. "Next she'll use his familiar knock."

We heard three loud raps. Shipman's grimace relaxed into a smile as he finally realized it was just Bonnie scaring us. He swept to the door like an usher and opened it grandly while bowing at the waist.

"Oh, do come in, Grand Earl of Haymeyer," he exulted, stopping short when he discovered it was indeed Earl after all. "Hey, Earl, I'm sorry, man," he said. "I wanted to see how the film looked and—"

"That's all right," Earl said, shocking us all. "I took her out to dinner."

We looked at each other. Earl didn't sound like himself. Here was a man who had reached the heights as a special investigator for high government officials, had helped crack some of the most celebrated murder cases in Chicago history—including one committed by Margo's mother and another in which Mrs. Franklin had been the victim—and had been wildly successful in his own small firm in just more than a year of operation.

The man is usually all business. He is crisp, to the

point, and impatient with ambiguities and people who speak in vague terms. And now he is guilty of it himself.

"You took *who* out to dinner?" Margo and I said in unison. Larry was puzzled too, but was in speechless relief that he had been pardoned.

"Paige," Earl said dreamily, his eyes not even focusing on us.

"Sit down, Earl," Shipman said. Earl just looked at him, then at each of us with a silly grin. Bonnie appeared in the doorway.

"Why don't you sit down and tell us all about it, Earl," she suggested.

He ignored her. "Paige Holiday," he said, as if we weren't there.

"I don't believe this," I said.

"Let me sit down," Earl said, passing up a chair right in front of him. He hoisted himself onto the darkroom counter and directly into a tray full of wash and three or four eight-by-tens Shipman had shot the day before. The wash cascaded out both sides of the tray and left Earl sitting heavily on the sticky prints, which were gluing themselves to his seat. He didn't notice a thing.

"I think," Bonnie said in great wisdom, "you'd better tell us about Paige Holiday."

"I'm in love," he said. "I'm going to marry her."

"Whoa!" Shipman whooped. "Does she know that?"

"Hm? Of course not. Unless she can tell how I feel about her."

"*We* sure can," I said. "So who is she? Where'd you

meet her? How long have you known her?"

When Haymeyer looked at his watch, Shipman decided, "There goes the business. He has to look at his watch to see how long he's known her, but the greatest detective mind since Columbo is going to marry her, posthaste!"

"About seven hours, I guess," Earl said, grinning again.

"So you met her at the rehab center," Margo said.

"Uh-huh."

"Tell us about her," Bonnie repeated.

"I did. She can't wait to meet you all."

"No, tell *us* about *her*."

"Uh-huh."

Bonnie looked at her watch. Her grown kids were coming for dinner, but she didn't want to miss this. Shipman fidgeted too, anxious to try to print from the dry negatives of the infrared experiment. Margo stared at Earl, as if hoping that a cautious silence would bring him out. I looked at Margo, remembering when I had been nearly incoherent about her.

"She's not real tall," Earl began. "She's not real skinny, nor is she overweight. She's sorta, I guess you'd call it, cuddly." We shot a collective doubletake.

"Well, I didn't cuddle her, of course. Yet."

"Earl!" Margo scolded.

"She has dark brown hair that hangs straight and is cut evenly at her shoulders. Her eyes are dark too, but they're deep and expressive, and it's as if she can look right past your face and into your brain. She's not any

11

less pretty when she's not smiling, but when she smiles it's as if she's happy from the shoulders up. She just breaks into these wise and knowing and open grins that make you feel like you've made her day.

"She loves Little Earl, and all the kids. They hardly respond to her, or to anybody, but she just keeps giving and giving anyway."

We were enraptured. I hadn't heard Earl go on so since he talked about his first stakeout. He was a detective's detective, and until now I wouldn't have thought anything else in life could matter to him as much as his work. He'd had a good marriage and just the one child, and when his wife died, he threw himself into his career as never before. He had hardly dated in seven years.

"At first she was just the new girl on the staff to me," Earl said. "You know how I am with new people. She introduced herself and told me about how Little Earl has been getting along. It was just small talk after that, but not to her. Even when I just mentioned the weather, she stared deep into my eyes and listened. And if I said anything remotely funny, she seemed to really enjoy it."

"That's neat," Shipman said, as if he meant it. I think it even embarrassed him that he was so moved by Earl's infatuation. "Uh, how old is she, Earl?"

"Oh, maybe a year or two older than I am," he said. "Maybe forty."

"Available?"

"A widow. Loves kids. Has none of her own. Lost one at birth."

12

"Sad."

"Yeah, but she's not. She's dealt with it, I guess. She's really at peace with herself."

Margo and I locked eyes for an instant, wondering if she might be a Christian.

"I'd like to meet this woman," I said. "I really would."

"Me too," Margo said.

"Paige," Earl said.

"Hm?"

"Not 'this woman.' Paige Holiday. Someday Paige Haymeyer. I took her to dinner."

"You said that. How was it?"

"I don't remember what I ordered."

"I mean, how was the time with Paige?"

"Outstanding." He was grinning again, and we were all amused. And pleased. And just half a hair wary. She sounded like a wonderful person, one of those rare birds that is an instant hit with everyone. But could she really be available? With no attachments? And might Earl get hurt by falling so hard so fast, especially considering his background, temperament, and years of detachment?

"So you're going to see her again next month?" I ventured.

"Next month? Tomorrow noon."

"Earl," Shipman said, "you've got a business to run."

"I know that. And it'll survive. I'll be the better for this, I can tell you that. It'll make me a better detective, a better boss, a better businessman—"

"Sure," Shipman said, "and it'll improve your golf game, your racquetball, and your breath."

"Particularly my breath," Earl said, almost coming back to reality. "I'm bound to be more conscious of that."

"It's never been a problem," Bonnie said too quickly, almost motherly. She blushed when we demanded to know why she was an expert on Earl's breath.

"Well, anyway, I'm back," Earl said. "And what're you all still doing here this late at night? I wanted to develop my infrared film and surprise you skeptics with it in the morning."

"Well, the negs are dry," Shipman said. "You wanna print some?"

"Tell me you didn't already develop the film, Ship," Haymeyer said, almost whining.

"I already told you I did," Larry said, incredulous.

"Did what?"

"Developed your stupid infrared film!"

"Oh, OK. Let's see what we've got."

As Earl slid down from the counter, the tray flipped over toward him and splashed him anew. "What's this?" he said, reaching for the photographs stuck to his pants.

I just had to meet this Paige Holiday.

Chapter Two

We all peered intently at the negatives until we were
convinced that Earl had been right, as usual. He had
turned out the lights and shut all his curtains the night
before, then shot a roll of film in the blackness while we
stood mostly hooting at him.

"This could revolutionize our work," he had pre-
dicted. Margo and I bet he would have a roll of black
ravens flying through an unlit coal mine. Shipman had
been silent, not eager to be wrong either way. When we
had told Bonnie about it the next morning, she advised
against doubting Earl and his new gadgets.

"So we were wrong," I was saying now. It was
obvious Earl and Shipman could pull decent photographs from the negatives. "Do we have to stay and
watch you print them, or can we come back later and see
the final product? We haven't eaten yet."

We dropped Bonnie off at her place—which was
within walking distance, except on dark nights—then
headed off to eat. When I brought Margo back to her car
at Earl's office later, she was too tired to even come up. I
lived in the building, so I was home. I kissed her good

night, and she left for her apartment in Winnetka, a few minutes away.

I had brought Shipman a sandwich, which Earl ate, even though he had been out to dinner with Paige. "Just thinking about her makes me hungry," he said, shaking his head. He still smelled of freshly developed pictures, probably because he still had the remnants of a couple of them stuck to his pants. Normally he was a pretty dapper guy.

"Where's the Ship?"

"Went home. He's been putting in a lot of hours for me lately. I could never pay him enough. You either."

"But I'm learning so much, Earl. So is Margo. I know it sounds strange to disagree with your employer when he says he can't pay you enough, but we both feel good about being here, and we're both addicted to this business. We think it's because we've been learning it from you."

"And Shipman. Don't think you don't pick up things from him everyday. Sometimes I think he's more of a natural than I am at parts of detective work." Earl paused.

I almost nodded.

"Don't agree with that," he said. "Wanna see the infrared prints?"

They were impressive. Nothing like you get with a flash, of course, but there were some fairly contrasty prints of Earl's furniture. "I wish I'd put one of you in the picture," he said. "It looks as if a person would be identifiable, doesn't it?"

16

"It really does. Wanna shoot me now?"

It was eerie, "posing" in pitch darkness and hearing the shutter click. Earl said he was too tired to develop the new shots that night. "But let's look at 'em tomorrow when I get back from seeing Paige." And with that he was off into his fantasy again. "I just flat want to talk about her," he said.

"This is so unlike you. You know that, don't you Earl? I mean, it's all right for you to fall in love, but you're like a high school kid. I never thought much about what it would be like if you found yourself a new love, but I know I never expected this."

"I never did either, kid. I never expected to fall in love again. I knew if it ever happened, it would have to come out of the blue and hit me over the head, because not only have I not been looking for it, I've been running the other way. I've made myself unavailable, and when I see a TV show or a movie and find myself envious of someone in love, I push it from my mind. I almost wish I could do that now, but this woman has me."

"She has you?"

"Yeah. And she doesn't even know it."

"You don't think she knows how you feel?"

"I know people pretty well, Philip. Maybe not women as much as men, but my guess is that she not only feels nothing for me, but that she also has no idea of what impact she made on me."

"What makes you think so?"

"She just seems selfless. Her whole being reaches out. She's a friend, a listener, an others-first person."

17

"Wow. I wish someone somewhere was saying that about me."

"Yeah, those are some attributes, aren't they?"

"What would she think if you told her how you feel?"

"It would really mess her up, Philip. I hardly know the woman."

"I know you've got ten years or more on me, Earl, and it's none of my business, but if you hardly know the woman, what makes you think you're in love with her?"

"I don't know. But it's so real it has to be true."

"That doesn't sound like Haymeyer reasoning."

"Don't you think I know that? There's no reason in this. The woman knocked me off my feet, and I can't quit thinking about her. Maybe I'll find out she's got green toes or likes bullfights or something, and I'll lose it. Meanwhile, I keep dreaming of her in my future. If she's half the woman I think she is, she's twice what I ever hoped for since Janice."

"What would Janice think?"

"She'd be thrilled. They're two of a kind in many ways. Janice was selfless, though I don't think she was as at ease with strangers as Paige is. You really need to see her in action. She's something. Just alive, glowing, brightening her space."

I thought of a song, but said nothing.

"I could keep you up all night talking about her," Earl said. "You'd better get to bed so you can be to work on time tomorrow."

"What's the difference?" I said. "I hear the boss has a heavy date and won't be in anyway."

18

"A cuddly date, anyway," Earl said. "And don't kid yourself. I'll be in before I leave to see her. No tellin' when I'll get back, though. Philip, this woman—ah, go to bed."

Earl began tidying the office, as he did every night. It wasn't that Bonnie was not organized. She was. In fact, her desk and area were always pin neat. But Earl is fastidious and a compulsive straightener. When he's working, his office—and ours—can be total messes. But before he leaves for his apartment, just a few steps down the hall on the second floor of his building, he gets the office into the shape he wants to see it when he arrives the next morning—always early.

An hour later, as I finished my reading and sketching and was crawling into bed, I realized I had not heard Earl lock up and head toward his place, two doors down from mine. I threw on a floor-length terry cloth robe and padded to the office, where lights still burned. It was nearly midnight.

I figured Earl must have felt he was too excited to sleep and had decided to process the film he had shot of me. I crept in toward the darkroom, but noticed the light on in his own office.

I hadn't intended to surprise him, but my slippers made no noise on the carpet, and I found myself standing in his doorway, undetected. He sat on the edge of his chair, elbows on his desk, face in his hands.

"Excuse me, Earl," I said, startling him slightly. "I just thought you might be in the darkroom."

"Nope," he said, quickly rubbing his face with both

19

hands. He had been crying. "Just leaving." He reached for his desk lamp and put us both in darkness.

"Don't try anything," he joked, his voice thick with emotion. "I have infrared eyes and can still see you." I didn't laugh, and he noticed. He put his arm around my shoulder and led me out to where the main office light was on. He wiped his face dry with his free hand.

"Philip, my man," he said, "you know that for all I think of you and Margo, I don't buy your religious thing. But right now"—and his voice began to break—"I feel so grateful to someone, that I just don't know who to thank."

"Grateful?"

"For Paige. Oh, I know it may never come to anything. But it's been so long since I've allowed myself to feel the stirrings, since I've been romantically interested in anyone. I had convinced myself that I would be better off shutting out that part of my life. Philip, if all I get out of this was today's thrill of adoring the woman Paige seems to be, it's enough to thank someone for."

I didn't know what to say. Should a person who doesn't really believe in God thank Him for a friendly, nice-looking woman who makes him feel good? She sounded like a Christian, but that didn't mean God was going to make a gift of her to Earl.

"I believe God is the author of all good things," I said, trying not to sound too pious or sermonic.

"Someone who knew what he was doing wrapped this package," Earl said. "I don't feel comfortable thanking

God for it, but I am grateful. What a wonderful feeling, to have been awakened after so many years."

I had never seen Earl emotional. Never. It was strange. And nice. Perhaps in spite of the bizarre nature of his feelings, he was actually getting things in perspective after falling in love virtually at first sight. He was talking a lot more now about how nothing may come of it—and that this day may be his only good memory—rather than that he was going to marry her, no ifs, ands, or buts.

"I don't think I'm going to sleep well tonight," he said.

"I will," I said. He clapped me on the back and locked the office door.

"See you bright and early," he said, the way he had done nearly every night for a year.

"Bright and early," I repeated.

Chapter Three

In truth, Earl enforced no regular hours on anyone except his secretary, Bonnie, who was to be in at eight and could leave anytime after four thirty unless there was an emergency. She usually stayed nearly as late as everyone else, sometimes into the early evening.

As for Larry and Margo and me, by midmorning Earl wanted us either in the office or out tracking down leads and sources for our individual assignments.

Larry and Earl had been working together on a suspected embezzlement ring at a big bank downtown, not far from where Larry lived. Shipman had gotten himself hired as a teller and made noises among his co-workers that he "could sure use some extra money," while Earl consulted with the executives and accountants to determine just how the siphoning off of funds was being done.

They felt they were close to something, and near the end of each working day, Bonnie, Margo, and I waited impatiently to hear of their progress.

Meanwhile, Margo was working on a welfare fraud case that came to Earl through his old friend and former

United States attorney—now Illinois governor—James A. Hanlon. It was Margo's first case alone, and she was doing well. She wasn't playing undercover or anything, just asking a lot of questions in the welfare office and among check recipients.

I had been assigned to investigate the mysterious death of a teenage boy. He had been an athlete, a good student, a leader in school and in his church, yet he had been run over by a truck and killed in the alley behind an X-rated bar on the city's west side. His father had hired us, presumably to clear his son's name.

"What I can't understand was the trace of alcohol found in his blood," the tearful father told us one night. "I think I can take it if you find that Justin was not the boy we thought he was. But I just have to know."

Earl warned me later, "Mr. Keith is not going to like what you find, but he's paying a lot of money for the truth, so give it to him straight."

"What do you think I'm gonna find? You know this kid or something?"

"Nope, and don't jump to any conclusions just because I do after so many years in this business. Go into it with an open mind, hoping you can tell the man that his kid was kidnaped, force-fed booze, and was killed when he tripped in the alley, leaving the porn shop after trying to preach to the customers. But don't be surprised if you find that the kid played his parents' game Sundays and during the week, then turned into a junior Mr. Hyde on Saturday nights."

Larry Shipman cut in. "Why not just tell the old

man what he wants to hear, regardless of what Philip finds? What would it hurt?"

"I couldn't do it," I said.

"And I wouldn't want him to, Ship, even though I know your motive is all right. Our whole business—the law itself—centers on truth. We can't let it erode, even around the edges, for whatever reason."

My investigation had led to Justin's best friend, a classmate people said had often been seen with the now dead boy. I would be interviewing him after school.

Strangely, after my midnight chat with Earl, I found myself awake at six o'clock the next morning. I usually need more sleep. I called Margo. She answered groggily on the fourth ring.

"Hey, you got to bed a lot earlier than I did last night," I said. "How come you're still asleep?"

"I'm not, hon, thanks to you. Anyway, I stayed up preparing for my interviews today. I think I'm onto something that could cost a few patronage workers their jobs. Anyway, what's up?"

"Wondered what you were doing for breakfast this morning."

Margo and I met at a place about midway between our apartments. Somehow she never looked like she had just got up. "How do you do it? I must look like I'm still in bed."

"I'm just full of natural sunshine," she teased, laughing.

"I'd love to wake up to your natural sunshine every

morning for the rest of my life," I said.

"You're going to, Philip. I'm wearing this huge rock you're still paying for, aren't I?"

"Then why don't we settle on a date?"

"We did. We're having one now. One I shouldn't have agreed to. Imagine a suitor waking me up and giving me an hour's notice for a date. You'd really have to love a guy to let him get away with that."

"You sure have strange ways of telling me you love me."

"You want me to stand on the table and tell the whole place? I would, you know."

"I'm sure you would, Margo. No need."

We prayed and ate, and she told me about her case. "The mistake the crooks in the welfare office made was that they chose stupid accomplices. First, they chose friends who lived not far from where they do. Then when I started asking questions, they warned their friends not to tell me anything. So, instead of playing innocent or confused, the accomplices tell me straight out, 'My friend at the welfare office told me not to tell you anything.'

"I asked one woman why she got five checks for varying amounts in one month. She told me the welfare office explained it to her and that it was all right, but she couldn't remember the reason. She's been getting those checks consolidated into one now for the last three months. It's a whopper each time."

"You got enough for Earl to bring in the state authorities?"

"I think so. After today I should have the names of everybody inside the department who had anything to do with it. The names of those who received the checks were easy. Many of them were going to the same address under different names.

"One man was so sad. He said that the welfare office worker who was paying him triple his usual amount had promised him he wouldn't have to split the money with her this month if he promised not to tell me anything. So he didn't tell me anything."

We both laughed. It was hard to tell who were the bumblers—the unsuspecting accomplices, or the idiots who chose them.

"It's really strange," I said, "but it appears that all the active cases we're on right now are coming to a boil at the same time. You'll have enough after today, Ship and Earl feel they're really close at the bank, and I could wrap up this Justin Keith thing today."

"Really? Was Earl right? Is the father not going to want to hear what you're going to tell him?"

"I don't know. Right now it looks rather encouraging. I still haven't pieced together the last night of his life, but every single person I've talked with, from relatives to other friends, to teachers, to girl friends, all vouch for the kid's character. He really *was* a nonsmoker, nondrinker, not a rowdy, not ashamed to stand up for what he thought was right, respected and obeyed his parents, everything."

"What do you make of it?"

"I'm not sure, but somehow this Brian Dahlberg

friend of his raises a lot of eyebrows when his name is mentioned. Justin's friends couldn't figure out that friendship. They couldn't imagine Brian having a lasting impact on Justin; they didn't seem a natural pair. Brian is a jock, like Justin, but he's a senior—a year older—and a rich kid. Has his own car, lots of stuff, lots of girls. He's known as a boozer and does drugs; nothing real hard, but definitely illegal. I'm anxious to talk to him."

"Let me know how it turns out."

I told Margo about my strange conversation with Earl the night before. She responded with silence. I let her think. Finally, she spoke. "Could it be that we've been right all along about Earl's tenderness? That's not the reaction of the tough, professional investigator, is it?"

"His head-over-heels bit wasn't, either," I said.

"No, but that's a little more understandable than that he would be moved to tears of gratitude for one idyllic day with a total stranger."

"He's going to see her for lunch today, you know."

"Yeah. What I wouldn't give to be a little mouse at that meal."

"Well, babe, no doubt we'll hear all we want to hear about it later," I said.

"And more."

"Right."

"Philip."

"Hm?"

"What do you think about the fact that all our cases are about to be wrapped up?"

"I think Earl will just pull all the stacked and waiting

ones out of his drawer and start assigning them."

"I know that. And I'm hoping he'll trust me with an important one again. But what I'm getting at is sort of superstitious, I guess."

"You mean that all our cases coming to a head at the same time means something big might be on the horizon for the agency, just like when a bunch of male babies are born, people think we're going to have a war?"

"Yeah."

"We're kind of a small staff to have a war."

"Oh, Philip, you know what I mean. It's Earl's style to tell clients right up front that their case may be in our pending file for a month or two, in case they want to take it elsewhere. I'm just wondering what'll happen if he gets involved with Paige and doesn't want to take any cases himself."

"It'll just mean more work for us."

"But you know that's not good. We need his input and his energy. We need his presence."

"You make him sound like God."

"We need His presence, too, but let's face it. Earl *is* the EH Detective Agency—in more than just name."

"Somehow I don't think he'll give up any good cases for his new love."

"Don't be too sure, Philip."

Earl looked bleary-eyed at the office. He was scurrying around, making phone calls, barking orders to Bonnie, and generally trying to wrap everything up so he could get to the rehab center to pick up Paige at noon.

The center was on his way downtown, and he had told Shipman that he would probably see him near the bank at the end of the working day.

"You look shot," I told him.

"Leave it to you for a cheery comment every morning," he said. "At least I look happy, don't I?" He turned toward Bonnie, who was eyeing him with wonder. "What do you think, Bon, should I tell Paige that I look this way because I had trouble sleeping last night?"

"She'll figure that," Bonnie said.

"But I'll tell her why," Earl said. "I'll tell her it's because of her."

"I wouldn't," Bonnie said. "Not if you don't want to scare her off."

"Your face will scare her off today," I said.

"Philip, you keep making cracks like that and you're gonna find out why I'm the only gumshoe in this office who has enough brains to carry a gun."

"Sorry, Earl. You really might want to splash some cold water in your face before you leave, though."

"What, and wake up? No way. As long as I'm dreaming, I might as well be asleep."

Bonnie shook her head. None of us had ever seen Earl like this. I mentioned to him that our cases all seemed to be nearing an end at the same time. "No kidding?" he said. "Maybe I should propose today, then put off starting the pending cases until we get back from our honeymoon."

He was laughing. Bonnie said, "I tell you not to even tell her why you couldn't sleep last night, and you want to propose today. Don't ask *me* for any more advice."

Earl packed his briefcase and gave the office one more glance. "You talked to this Dahlberg yet?"

"After school today. He gets out at one thirty."

"Has he seen you yet? Know who you are, I mean?"

"Nope."

"You know who he is?"

"By pictures and make of car."

"Why don't you see if you can watch him at lunchtime? Might give you an idea of what he's like, who he runs with, that kind of thing."

With that, Earl was gone. Bonnie and I shrugged. "He still thinks business occasionally," she said.

"And when he does, he's right on the money," I said. I called the school to find out when the lunch breaks were, then drove to Skokie South and cruised the parking lot until I found the black Pontiac Trans Am with Brian Dahlberg's father's license number.

I parked two rows away where I had a perfect view, and sat waiting.

Chapter Four

At about noon, just when Earl was probably opening his car door for Paige Holiday, when Margo was probably making the last of her notes from her morning interviews, and when Shipman was trying to get next to his fellow "employees" at the bank in Chicago, I saw a tall, loping, good-looking blond kid get into the Trans Am and start the engine.

He was alone, and I was surprised. He was supposed to be everyone's friend, a guy with a girl on each arm. He was supposed to be a less-than-model driver as well, though his father had paid off five of his last six violation citations. Today he was driving like a gentleman.

That made him easier to follow without being obvious. I hung back a half block and even let other cars get between him and me. He drove about two miles, away from the usual haunts of the Skokie South kids. He pulled into a crowded fast food place and stood in a long line. He stared at the floor.

I wheeled over next to his car, then stood in the same line. He placed a very small order for a big kid, went outside, and sat on a cement bench. I took my meal to a window seat and watched him from inside. It took him longer to finish a cheeseburger and a small Coke than it did me to finish twice as much.

He hardly moved, eating as if in a trance. It didn't appear drug-induced or anything. His eyes were clear and his body steady, but he looked tired, and sad. He was not at all what I had expected. A guy and two girls greeted him on their way out, eager to stop and chat, but he just pursed his lips and nodded at them, unsmiling, and they moved on.

When he stood and headed for his car I hurried to dump my trash and catch up with him. Just as he put the key in his door, I said, "Brian? Are you Brian Dahlberg?"

"Depends," he said slowly.

"I'm Philip Spence. I have an appointment with you at one thirty."

"Yeah, hi. It's not one thirty, is it?"

"No, but I just wondered if we could talk now. Will you get in trouble if you miss your last class?"

"Nah. I was going to cut it anyway so I'd be home in time to see you. Wanna follow me there?"

We had his parents' mansion to ourselves. "Housekeeper comes at two, but she won't bother us. C'mon up to my room."

The house was beautiful. His room was huge, easily accommodating a king-size bed, a console color television, a wall stereo unit, and even a pinball machine. "Play if you want," he said, flopping on the bed. I shook my head.

34

"You've even got a CB unit in your bedroom," I said, knowing I sounded like a hick.

"Haven't used it in months. It was sort of a status thing for my dad. One of my friends' dad told my dad he had bought his kid one for his room; next thing I knew, I had one. Dumb. I listened to it for a few nights and got tired of it. Never asked for it. Never asked for any of this junk."

"I want to talk about Justin," I said.

Brian rolled up onto one elbow and pointed to a chair. As I sat down he covered his mouth with one hand and breathed deeply through his nose. He said nothing.

"Justin Keith," I said.

He nodded. "Yeah, I know."

"How come you suppose no one knew where he was that night he died?"

Brian glanced up at me, deep into my eyes. He appeared almost puzzled.

"None of my other contacts had any idea where he was or who he was with that night, except his mother. She said he said he was going downtown with you, maybe to a movie or something."

"Why didn't you believe her?"

"I did. That's why I'm here. But she said you denied it the next day. She said you said you were home all evening doing your homework and that your father vouched for you."

"So that's it then, huh?"

"No, that's not it then. Your father didn't get back into town from a business trip until midnight that night. Your mother could have vouched for you, but she didn't. She doesn't remember where you were."

"But you figure I was with him."

"Yeah. Because he doesn't lie."

"No, you're right about that. He doesn't. Didn't. I can't get into any trouble unless I had something to do with his death, right?"

"Right."

"Well, I didn't have anything to do with it, except—"

"Except?"

"Except I got us into the place. I had the fake IDs. I talked us into there. I egged him on. I made the dare, and I even made him a deal."

"A deal?"

"I wanted to see how real the kid was. He was the only really straight-arrow type of a guy I had ever spent much time with. I liked him a lot. He kept wanting me to go with him to picnics with his family. Can you imagine? A picnic with *family?* And he wanted me to go to church with him. I couldn't believe it.

"He never hassled me about getting loaded or drinking or anything, but he never joined in. He even got me to see a couple of G-rated pictures. I hadn't seen one since I took my niece to *The Black Stallion*. He never wanted to see the kind of movies I wanted to see. Maybe he wanted to, but he felt he shouldn't. I played upon his naiveté. I finally talked him into it."

"Why are you telling me this?" I asked. "Only because you weren't directly involved in his death and know you can't get in trouble?"

"No, I would have told you anyway," he said, his breath short and his eyes darting. "I've lived with it for weeks, and I feel like a creep." He hung his head. "I *am* a creep. I ruined a perfectly good kid, just because I had nothing better to do. Do you know Justin excelled at things money could never buy? I can compete because my dad makes a lot of money. I can get by as a mediocre athlete and a crummy student. But why was Justin a good kid and a good student? Because he was, that's all. It was him. It came from inside, not from anybody's wallet."

Brian lay back and put his hands behind his head. "I don't care who knows. In fact, I *want* my parents to know. I want you to tell anyone you want." He swore.

"You wanna tell me about that night?"

"There's not much to it," he said. "I told Justin that if he was so concerned about my experiencing his kind of life, he ought to experience mine. We went to a straight movie, and then I took him to the X-rated place. I don't believe he ever drank before. I convinced him the bouncer would really be mad if he didn't drink and that we would either have to pay a lot of money or not be allowed to leave. The place really spooked him."

"Where was he going when he was hit by the truck in the alley?"

"To the bathroom. I pointed him down the hall, but he missed the door and staggered out into the alley. He was sick."

"The driver says he thought Justin saw him, but when he backed up, Justin stepped behind the truck."

"I know," Brian said. "I was so jealous of that kid."

"You mean of his life-style?"

"I suppose. But I never got close enough to figure out what made him tick. I'm more jealous of him now than ever."

"Now?"

"That's right. Now."

The boy rolled over onto his stomach and hid his face in a pillow. He wasn't crying. I guessed it had been a long time since Brian Dahlberg had cried about anything. I waited a few minutes.

"I want you to do something for me," I said. "When you're up to it."

"What's that?" he said from behind the pillow.

"I want you to tell Justin's parents what you told me."

He sat up and let his legs dangle off the side of the bed. "I don't know if I can do that," he said. "They'll hold me responsible. And they'll be disappointed in him, too."

"I don't think they will, Brian," I said. "Do you know what it looks like as it stands? Like he was a liar who went for some kicks and wound up getting himself killed."

"In other words, his father is worried about the family name?"

"No, his father doesn't care about his own reputation. He cares only about his son's, and about his own peace of mind. He thought he knew his son, and now he isn't so sure."

"He thought he knew his own son?"

"That sound strange to you?"

"Doesn't it to you?"

I didn't respond.

Brian sat seemingly on the verge of tears for several minutes. "So, you want me to make it clear to Justin's parents that he was all they hoped he would be, but that I was the creep they were afraid he might have become."

"I wouldn't put it that way."

"I would. And I will. They need to know."

"Should I get your parents' permission first?"

"Are you kidding? My dad would kill me. As it is, they'll want to leave town."

"I don't have any authority to ask you to do this, you know. I can simply tell the parents what I learned and ask them to keep it quiet. No one ever has to know."

"Then why do you want me to do it?"

"For the same reason you want to do it. The same reason that drove you to tell me when you didn't have to. You were looking for someone to confess to. You'd had enough of the sham. You live with *this* sham every day," I said, waving at the room. "I was easy. You knew I couldn't hurt you, and you had to tell someone. How about having some guts? Tell someone who isn't easy to tell. Tell someone who could tell others to protect his son's reputation. Tell someone who could ruin your— and your father's—reputation.

"But remember, you do it on your own. No laying it off on me. My job is finished. I found what I needed to find. I'll go back to my office and file a report with my boss. He'll trade it to Mr. Keith for more money than a little running around and asking questions is worth, and we can all go our merry ways."

We sat staring at each other.

I passed the housekeeper on my way out.

Chapter Five

By the time I got back to the office, Margo was there typing up her report for Earl. "Wrapped it, huh?" I said, but she was so into her work that she just stuck out her hand without looking up. I squeezed it as I walked by.

Bonnie was on the phone and mouthed, "Larry," to me, making me stop. She covered the mouthpiece. "He's really onto something big and wants me to get to Earl right away." She turned back to the conversation. "I'll do what I can, Larry." She never called him Ship or Shipman. Not even *Mr.* Shipman.

"What's up?" I asked when she hung up.

"Larry called on his break from a pay phone down the street. He says the accomplices at his level in the bank have let on that the real leader in the scam is high in the corporate structure." She was dialing.

"You mean maybe even someone Earl has been working with in trying to break the thing?"

"Hello, this is the EH Detective Agency calling for Mr. Earl Haymeyer; I believe he's with Mrs. Paige Holiday . . . Thank you." She covered the phone. "That's right, Philip. Luckily, no one but the chairman of the board even knows that Earl has a man working inside." I started to respond, but she quieted me with a finger. "Oh, they're not. Well, would you have him call his office immediately when they return? Thank you."

"Hope Earl doesn't get her in trouble with her superiors," Bonnie told me. "They expected her back at two.

"By the way, Earl asked me to give you these," Bonnie said, handing me a manila envelope.

I took it back to my desk, held it in my teeth while taking my coat off, then slid the contents out. "Ah, the pictures from last night. Have you seen 'em, Bonnie?"

She nodded, but now Margo was out of her trance. "*I* haven't! May I?" She gathered up her rough draft, made a few scratches on it, asked Bonnie to type the final version for her, and hustled back to my desk.

"I don't believe this," she said, staring at the grainy, high contrast black and white prints. "It's not even difficult to tell who it is. It's incredible. Where were these taken? That looks like my desk in the background."

"It is. I was standing right where you are, and there wasn't a light on in the place—not even out in the hall."

Margo leafed through the photos, letting out a faint whistle between her teeth, "Maybe this *will* revolutionize our work." The phone rang.

"If that's Earl, I want to talk to him," I said.

"Me too," Margo said.

"Who may I say is calling? . . One moment please. Philip, it's a young man named Brian?"

"Thanks, Bonnie. I'll talk to you in a minute, Margo," I said, punching Brian onto my line. "Brian, how ya doin'?" I began, trying not to sound too eager.

"I'm not doin' too well, Spence," he said, "but I know what I have to do. What I want to know is, Will you set it up and go with me?"

"You want me to talk to the Keiths?"

"Yeah."

"I think I can do that. You ready to do it tonight? They'll probably be anxious."

"I guess I'd better do it now before I change my mind."

"Hey, Brian?"

"Yeah."

"You're doing the right thing, you know that?"

"I think I do."

"I'll call you back."

I rummaged around to find the Keith file and called their home. Mrs. Keith said she would call her husband at work and get back to me if there was any problem; otherwise she would plan on seeing us at seven. While I was dialing Brian to let him know, I heard Bonnie taking Earl's call. "Remember I want to talk to him," I hollered just as Brian answered.

"It's all set for tonight at seven, guy," I said.

"Could I ask one more favor, Mr. Spence?"

"Sure, and call me Philip."

"Yeah, Philip, would you mind driving too much?"

"Uh, no."

"I mean I just don't want to pull up—or drive away

43

later—in my Trans; you know what I mean?"

"Yeah. I'll pick you up at six forty-five."

When I hung up, Bonnie was already off the phone. "I needed to talk to him," I reminded her.

"I know, but you'll get your chance. He's going by the bank around closing time to pick up Larry down the street. He wants you to meet him down there and to bring his tape recorder—"

"But I have to be back here in time to—"

"I know, Philip. I told him you seemed to be arranging something for this evening, and he said he was sure you could drop off his tape recorder if you hurried. I also told him that Margo had finished her assignment, and he said she should feel free to come along."

"Let me," Margo said. "I want to tell you about my day."

"Let you? Let's get going. Earl forgot about the traffic at this time of day, and I have to get right back."

Bonnie brought me Earl's metal tape recorder case. "Fresh tapes, batteries, and everything," she said, like a mother handing out lunch boxes at the beginning of the day. "Meet Earl and Larry at State and Randolph."

I didn't give Margo much of a chance to tell me about her day, though she did work in that she found more of the same information she had turned up before and felt she had solid cases against everyone she had determined was involved.

"It'll make Governor Hanlon look good, cleaning his own house, and it will make Earl look good to him

44

again, as if he needed that," Margo said.

"As if *we* needed that," I corrected. "The gov will just try to steal him away for a state job again."

By the time I had brought Margo up to date on the Keith-Dahlberg deal, we were off the expressway and into the Loop. Earl and Larry were in Earl's car, parked at a meter. Margo tooled around the block while I dashed over with the tape recorder.

"I wanted the camera, Philip," Earl said. "Not the tape recorder."

I just about died. "You've got to be kidding," I said.

"I am," Earl said, and they both cracked up.

"You guys got nothing better to do than sit here thinking of ways to give me heart failure?"

"As a matter of fact, we do. We have an appointment with the bank officers for dinner tonight, from the chairman of the board through the president, the senior executive vice president, and all the rest. Including, I might add, the man behind this whole scheme."

"Why was he dumb enough to involve people at the teller level?" I asked.

"I wouldn't know," Earl said. "But I think the rest of the executive committee is clean. Maybe he knew he could never find help there and was afraid to try anyone else. There's Margo. You'd better go. I'll be anxious to hear about your talk with Dahlberg—"

"And with Dahlberg *and* the Keiths tonight," I said.

"No kidding? I'm anxious to read Margo's report, too. Now get going."

"How was Paige today?"

45

"Get outa here!" Shipman interrupted. "We don't have time for all that!"

Margo had passed but was waiting at a light. I jumped in just as it turned green, and she fought the traffic all the way back to Glencoe, arriving just in time to have sandwiches with Bonnie, ordered from the deli down the street. I kept glancing at my watch.

"What are you two going to do tonight?" I asked.

"I don't want to get too far from here with all the news you three will be bringing back," Bonnie said. "What time is Earl's meeting?"

"He didn't say, but it's for dinner. I don't know exactly what he's planning or why he wanted the tape recorder, so I can't tell you when they'll get back. If you two want to be close, you could stay in my apartment so you'll know when any of us get back."

Bonnie said she had some reading she wanted to get done, and Margo wanted to study for a night school course in criminology, so they took me up on my offer. "You'd better get going," Bonnie said.

Brian was waiting for me in front of his home. He wore a short jacket, and his hands were thrust into his jeans pockets, thumbs sticking out. He slid into the car and asked me not to leave yet. I put the car in park. "We've got a few minutes," I said. "If you want to talk."

He said nothing. He just sat. Once he glanced expectantly at me as if to ask if I had any last-minute advice. I didn't. He buried his face in his hands and

46

breathed deeply, then wiped his mouth with one hand while turning to stare out the window at nothing. "OK, let's go," he said.

We arrived at the modest Keith home right at seven, and I had locked and shut my door before realizing that Brian was still in the car. I walked around to his side. The front porch light was on. I saw movement through the picture window. Brian stared straight ahead.

I leaned up against the car as if in no hurry, but after a minute I opened his door. "I'm not going to force you," I said. "But you're this far."

He looked up at me. "This sure isn't going to be easy."

I nodded. He stepped from the car and started up the walk ahead of me.

Chapter Six

Mrs. Keith opened the door before Brian could ring the bell. I looked past her and saw her husband waiting on the couch in the living room, still in his business suit.

"Brian, please come in," Mrs. Keith said warmly. "And you must be Mr. Spence."

She took our coats and led us to the living room where we exchanged greetings with Mr. Keith. He and his wife both had that hollow, dark-eyed look of the recently bereaved. They were pleasant enough, but guarded and curious. Brian asked about their two young daughters and the dog, and Mr. Keith appeared a bit agitated, anxious to get to the point.

After an embarrassing silence, I said, "Brian has come to talk to you tonight of his own accord. It won't be easy for him, but I think he realizes that his discomfort in no way matches your grief. I'll let him tell you in his own way whatever he wants."

Brian suddenly became concerned with straightening a strand in the shag carpet with his foot. "I, uh, I want to tell you of the impact your son had on me," he said finally. "And then I want to tell you of the impact I had on him." He fidgeted, and Mr. Keith interrupted.

"Justin never thought he made any impact on you, as much as he tried." Mrs. Keith shushed him with a wave.

"I know, I know that," Brian said quickly. "That may have been true at first, but not totally."

It took him twenty minutes to tell the Keiths the story of a strange friendship between a middle-income, straitlaced kid, who broke into the "in" crowd because of good grades and athletic skills, and a dope-doing, not-caring, Cain-raising rich kid.

"I could never figure him," Brian said. "I kept thinking that if I could just get through to him, he'd see he was missing out on all the fun in life. When I finally realized he had everything and was everything that I had always wanted deep down, it was hard to admit, even to myself. I never told him; in fact, I got a little angry with him.

"He kept asking me to join his kinds of activities, family-type stuff, church, picnics, all that. I made a deal with him. I told him he would have to try my life-style first, then I would try his."

"That doesn't sound like the kind of a deal Justin would make," Mr. Keith broke in.

"You're right. I must have finally gotten to him on a night when his resistance was low. I didn't even tell him my plan. I just dragged him along. It was the first time he had ever let me take him anywhere he didn't really want to go."

"And the last time," Mr. Keith said coldly.

Brian stared at him and fell silent. When he spoke

again, his voice was thick. "Anyway, he hardly had anything to drink. It made him woozy and sick. I pointed him to the bathroom, but he went right out the back door and into the alley. Maybe he was thinking of just getting out. The next thing I heard was that a kid had been run over, and I just split."

Brian put both hands on his head. "That bothers me more than anything, that I just left him there. I knew no one in a place like that would tell anyone who they had seen with him. In fact, they probably denied he'd even been in the place."

I nodded.

"Anyway," Brian said, struggling to speak, "I wanted you to know that he loved you. And—and that he was everything you thought he was. And that I feel horrible for having forced him to do something he didn't want to do. I know his death was an accident, but I don't think he would have been hit if he hadn't been sick from the booze." Brian clasped a hand over his mouth to keep from sobbing.

Mr. Keith pursed his lips tightly while his wife let tears roll silently down her cheeks. "It's not a nice story, Brian," the man said, his grief tinged with anger. "But it helps to know what you've told us."

"I feel responsible," Brian blurted.

Mr. Keith rose from the couch, a tall, angular, imposing man. He strode past Brian to a cold fireplace. "You *are* responsible," he said, a little too loudly.

Brian was stunned. "I'm sorry," he said, "and I want you to forgive me." The words sounded strange coming from the boy, as if they had never before passed his lips or even crossed his mind.

"I want to forgive you," Mr. Keith said. "With everything that's in me, I *need* to forgive you. Justin was wrong. I wish he could have resisted you. But he was younger. He idolized you."

Brian looked genuinely surprised. "I idolized *him*," he said, his eyes finally moistening.

"Well, you had everything you wanted, you were popular, you answered to no one. He thought you were worldly-wise, and you were."

Mrs. Keith cried openly now. Brian wiped his eyes and stood. He looked vulnerable and weak, despite his youth and size. "Will you forgive me?" he said.

"I don't know," Mr. Keith said. "Do you think we'll feel any better letting you walk out of here with a weight off your shoulders? Is the weight you drop going to fill the void in our guts? Our son is gone, boy. I need to forgive you for *our* sake, not yours."

"I understand," Brian said desperately. "I'd do anything to turn the clock back."

Mr. Keith looked to his wife, who looked as if she wanted to speak. "I have an idea," she managed, looking sympathetically at the boy and speaking carefully.

"It's not our place to forgive you. We can't exonerate you. And telling you everything is all right now will not bring our son back. Neither will it change you. Your memory of this will fade much more quickly than ours—"

Brian tried to protest, but she kept talking. "It simply will, that's all. It's only natural. You will go on not having to answer for anything. You may take more drugs and be irresponsible—"

"I've done no dope since Justin died."

"I suppose that's good. Anyway, Brian, you made a deal, and I'm going to insist that you keep your part of it."

Brian looked quizzically at me, and I raised my eyebrows. The woman continued. "You said Justin had to sample your life-style before you would sample his. He did, and it cost him his life. Now you should sample his. It may cost you parts of your life."

"What are you saying, Mrs. Keith?" Brian asked.

"I'm saying that the Keith family is ready to return to some semblance of normalcy. We will never forget our son, and right now I can't imagine ever even being able to stop grieving over him. But now that our minds have been put at ease about his own character, and we can piece together the events before his death—and yes, we can even put some of the blame on you—I think the best thing for me and my husband and our girls is to get back to the things that made us such a close-knit family when Justin was with us."

Mr. Keith was obviously puzzled. "What are you driving at, honey?" he said kindly.

"Family activities, church socials, outings, picnics, ball games. We've virtually forced the girls to do nothing the last several weeks while we sat around feeling sorry for ourselves."

"We haven't felt sorry for ourselves as much as we worried that Justin had been something we thought he wasn't," Mr. Keith said.

"I know, but we're at the point now where we must go on. We must live our lives in such a way that our daughters aren't crippled by this."

"Granted, but what does it have to do with Brian and his deal with Justin?"

"I'm going to invite him to go with us. I'm going to invite him so often that he'll have every chance he wants to fulfill his part of the bargain. And when he's had enough, he can just tell me or quit taking my calls. How about it, Brian?"

Before Brian could answer, Mr. Keith broke in. "Are you suggesting that the first time I try to loosen up in weeks, the first time I take my family out to the park where I taught my boy to catch a ball and throw a Frisbee, that I have to take along the boy responsible for his death?"

We all sat in silence. Mrs. Keith finally spoke to Brian, but it was for her husband's benefit. "Justin's dad will regret he said that in a little while. He'll realize how cruel it was and how much it took for you to come here tonight. He'll think about the fact that it will be just as painful for us to go on family outings with or without you now that Justin is gone. And he'll probably call you and invite you himself."

Brian shook his head slowly. "You know, Mr. Keith, I can forgive you for saying that, because it's the type of thing I would say if I were you. In fact, I would have said a lot worse, and I appreciate that you haven't done that. You know, when Justin first asked me to come with him to various family things, I couldn't think of anything I'd less rather do. I envied his relationship with you, but a softball game on a Saturday afternoon, when there were cars and girls and highs? Not for me. But right now I'd rather do that than anything I can think of. I can't guarantee it will change me or make me like Justin, and I'm not even sure that's what I want."

"But you do want to at least uphold your end of the deal, don't you?" Mrs. Keith said.

"You bet I do," Brian said, without emotion.

Something made me wish that the Keiths had evidenced more that would have given me the courage to ask them straight out if they were Christians. But they had not referred to God or Christ, and though I knew they were churchgoers, I didn't feel free to talk to them about it in front of Brian.

Mr. Keith leaned back on the couch and let his head fall back. As he stared at the ceiling, he began to cry softly. "Thank you for coming, Brian," he said, his voice strained because of the position of his neck. "We'll talk, huh?"

"Yeah," Brain said. "We'll talk."

Mrs. Keith saw us to the door. "I'd like to call on you again and chat sometime myself," I said. "Do you think that would be all right?"

"Surely, anytime."

Earl had warned me before about my penchant for wanting to "talk religion" to all my clients. My real

55

target was Earl, because I figured if he could ever see his need for Christ, he might not scold me every time word got back that I had, as he always says, "mixed business with religion."

"It's not religion," I always tell him. "And it doesn't need to mix with anything. The people we deal with have needs."

"And we have intelligent, rational, scientific answers for them," he always says.

"Not for all of them, Earl. There are some needs that can't be met by the greatest detection techniques ever devised." But I never wanted to push it. Margo and I had prayed a lot and laid a lot of groundwork with Earl. Too much, in fact, to risk blowing it by being disrespectful or insubordinate. I had confined my "religion" to my own time, especially when I wanted to talk to one of our clients.

"Hey, Brian, I'm proud of you," I said, pulling up to his house.

"Yeah, well, I dunno," he said.

"Could we get together sometime for a Coke or something?"

"Sure, if you want. I'm no prize for a buddy, you know."

"I know," I said, punching him in the shoulder. "But listen, take the Keiths up on their offer."

"*Her* offer."

"Right. But do it."

"If I go on picnics with them and for Cokes with you, I'll have made more friends from this than I've lost."

"You just might be right."

I felt like telling him that I would be praying for him, but it just didn't seem right.

"I'll be thinking about you," I said.

"You will?"

"I will."

"Thanks. Me too."

Bonnie was napping when Margo answered my knock. I kissed her. "Heard from Earl and Larry yet?"

"No. How'd your meeting go?"

"Really something," I said.

We decided to leave Bonnie a note and talk in the car so we wouldn't bother her. Margo was strangely silent when I finished my story. She usually had a bundle of reactions.

"What are you thinking?" I asked.

"That you should have struck while the iron was hot."

"You mean talked to them about Christ?"

"At least to Brian. He sounds like he could really be open."

"Brian's problems aren't drugs," I said. "They aren't even money or attitude. Those are just symptoms. He needs an anchor, a right relationship with his universe."

"Exactly my point, Philip. Why don't you think he's ready?"

"It's just that some people need to be brought up to a place of higher receptivity," I said. "You can't just hit 'em cold. Even you needed to come up to receptivity from point zero, remember?"

"Philip, you're pontificating. You sure hinted enough about what you had to offer—if I would only give you a chance to tell me—that I at least wanted to hear it. What have you said to Brian to whet his appetite?"

"Nothing, really. But I *will* get back to him. Hey, here's Earl. Let's wake up Bonnie."

Chapter Seven

Margo ran upstairs to rouse Bonnie while I greeted Earl as he emerged from his car. "You look whipped," I said. "Where's Larry?"

"He lives so close to where we were that he just went home. Anyway, I got it all on tape, so you won't miss anything. Wait till you hear it tomorrow."

"Tomorrow! I'll save *my* story till tomorrow, but we've been waiting all evening. C'mon, we'll make you coffee or whatever you need, but you're gonna tell us tonight."

Earl smiled wearily and shook his head. "It wasn't that long ago I was just as crazy as you."

I helped him carry his stuff upstairs and suggested we meet in my apartment rather than the office so we'd be more comfortable. Margo sat on the edge of the bed where Bonnie still lounged under an afghan. Earl sat in my easy chair. I served him coffee and set a TV tray in front of him for the tape recorder. Then I flopped onto the floor with my back against the wall.

Earl checked his watch and said he was good for only about another hour. "I'm seeing Paige tomorrow morning." We all smiled and caught each other's glances.

"When are *we* going to meet her?" Bonnie asked.

"Tomorrow. She and I are having breakfast, and I'm giving my tired and successful troops the day off, on one condition."

"What's the condition?" Margo asked.

"That you meet Paige and me for a picnic in the afternoon."

We all liked the idea, but we were soon bugging Earl in unison to get on with the tape. He introduced it:

"Ship had finally gotten next to the tellers who were involved with the removal of the cash each day. They trusted him enough to offer him a cut in exchange for his help, but they said their top-level contact would not approve bringing anyone new into the picture, so they weren't going to tell him. Like the idiots they are, though, they told Larry who their man was: none other than J. Michael Lucas, vice president in charge of customer relations. How ironic is that?"

"Unbelievable. So he was at this dinner tonight?"

"Sure was. And at first he didn't recognize Larry from the bank. When he did, he about dropped his teeth. You know Ship. Every time he caught the old man staring at him, he gave him a nod and a huge grin. Lucas just picked at his food, no doubt praying that if Larry was with me, he had not turned up anything that would implicate him in the embezzlement.

"I asked the chairman of the board if he minded if we taped the meeting. He said he didn't, so the first thing on the machine is the end of his permission. You'll catch a lot of miscellaneous pleasantries and table noises, but when the meeting gets going in earnest, you'll be able to make it out, I think."

Earl pushed the "play" button.

". . . no problem at all, though I assume it will become our property once your investigation is over."

"Certainly, sir. I record these just for my own information and will have no use for them once our dealings are finished."

The chairman of the board, in effect, brought the meeting to an order. "Gentlemen, please, I think we'd like to let Mr. Haymeyer tell us about the progress he and his staff have made in our behalf. He called this meeting, so we're hoping for good news and an end to our problem. Mr. Haymeyer."

"Yes, thank you. You men have not been aware that while I have been meeting with you over the past few weeks I had a member of my staff working in the bank. Your board chairman was the only one who knew this.

"Some of you may have realized when you were introduced to Mr. Shipman tonight that you had seen him at the teller windows recently. He is a member of my staff, and he's been working undercover in your behalf. I'm pleased to say that his findings have in many ways corroborated mine, and also that his findings have confirmed many of your own suspicions.

"Both Mr. Williams and Mr. Bennett, I believe, speculated that the problem revolved around the teller area and that cash seemed to be disappearing despite balanced books at the end of each day. When you men quizzed them, the tellers' stories were always the same; and they pledged their undying loyalty and interest in finding the culprits.

"Gentlemen, I believe Mr. Shipman has found the culprits. You'll be happy to know that while it involves four tellers, it involves no others at that level."

Earl turned the machine off. "I stole a look at Mr. Lucas here," he told us, "and he had begun to breathe again. I think he thought I was implying that we believed the problem began and ended with the four tellers, and of course that's what I wanted him to think." He turned the machine back on.

"Many of you gentlemen may be hard pressed to name all the tellers in the bank, but let me pass around this list of the names of the four, in case you might know any or all of them by name."

The chairman of the board spoke. "I want you men to know that Mr. Haymeyer and I have discussed at length what we would do if and when we tracked down those responsible for this, and I call it a travesty. As you know, I am very much concerned with the public trust. It's all a bank has to sell itself on, that and courteous service.

"It would not be in the best interests of our bank to prosecute these three men and this woman, because the police records are public domain. There would be no way to compute the potential damage to our business if word got out that we prosecuted four of our tellers for embezzlement. Our plan is to give these people the option of paying back the money in exchange for their being allowed to simply resign."

Earl spoke again. "Of course, we have plenty of evidence, and Mr. Shipman here is prepared to swear in court to what he has seen and heard, so should any of the four choose to put up a fight, the bank would win. I believe the guilty parties will see the light if we apply enough pressure, and I'm confident they will acquiesce."

Earl turned the tape off. "Right about at this point, the list of the four names got around to Lucas, and he studied them as if trying to put faces with the names. As he passed the note on he said something to the effect that he didn't really know any of them well, except maybe one. Then I began to lay the trap for him."

The tape came back in midsentence. Earl was speaking. ". . . if you have not already thought of it, you will. There is the real likelihood here that the news will get around the bank, among the other employees I mean, that four people are suddenly gone and the embezzling problem is over. They will begin to put two and two together, and you know the grapevine. Is there a way we can help? What will be your plan in dealing with this?"

The chairman of the board responded: "We may be forced to tell the whole story to our personnel and simply ask their assistance in keeping the lid on it."

"Maybe," Earl said. "You may have no choice. But one of the things they'll be extremely interested in is the disposition of the guilty. If they learn that these people got away with paying back the money and going free, you may have an internal public relations problem. And those kinds of problems always seem to leak outside to the public. Then you've got a *real* PR problem."

Margo and Bonnie and I grinned and pointed at Earl, seeing what he was up to. The chairman of the board's voice came on the tape: "Mike, what do you think? What would you do in that situation?"

J. Michael Lucas cleared his throat and his voice cracked. "Well, I, well, I agree that this would be unfortunate, and something we would want to avoid at all costs." It was almost as if he realized that once he got rolling he sounded all right, so he began to pick up confidence and steam. "In fact, I think it would be appropriate to let it be known that we have warned these people not to try to remain in the banking business and that even if they should resign and cooperate with us in a payoff plan, this does not insure them against an unfavorable reference from us should they seek future employment."

"We might have a legal problem there, Mike," a voice said.

"That's the personnel director," Earl explained.

"Unless we had it in writing that it was part of the deal, we could be sued for casting aspersions on someone who has not been convicted of a crime."

"But we're being *kind* in not prosecuting them!" Lucas insisted. "They owe it to us to not try to use us as a reference. And that would virtually keep them out of the banking field."

"Which you feel is just," Haymeyer said.

"Absolutely," J. Michael said.

"And what would your reactions be, gentlemen, if

64

someone at a higher level than teller had been involved in something like this?"

"That would be an entirely different story altogether," the personnel man said.

"Yes," the chairman said. "I believe I would be extremely interested in cleaning our own house, even to the point of prosecuting. There might be a temporary PR threat, but in the long run we'd be the better for it. We'd show that we are not above dealing with our own problems and demanding that men who have high positions of trust live up to their commitments. Wouldn't you agree, Mike? I mean, this is just as important an issue in customer relations, wouldn't you say?"

"Oh, even more so, sir. I agree wholeheartedly. We should spare no expense in that type of a situation. Tellers are gnats on a cow's back, but executives are, they are, uh—"

"We are the cows," the chairman said, obviously proud of himself and drawing laughter all around.

"Was Lucas laughing?" I asked.

"Not really," Earl said. "I was staring right at him." The laughter died, and the conversation continued. Earl was speaking. "Mr. Chairman," he said, "and members of the executive committee, I give to you the cow."

There was silence. "I gestured toward Mr. Lucas," Earl said. We heard gasps. "Lucas said nothing, he just blushed and glowered at me," Earl said. "Listen now. I'm talking to the chairman here."

There was not even a hint of any other noise. "Sir, I normally would consider it cruel to implicate a man in front of his colleagues, even if I were sure that he was in on such a crime—which I *am* sure of, by the way. But in this case, where Mr. Lucas has continually acted pompous and self-righteous, as he has evidenced even here tonight while his four young, sacrificial (albeit guilty) accomplices' careers come to an end, well, I just wanted to give him a chance to speak for himself. You helped me do that, sir, when I cued you to the PR questions. Past this point—after turning over to you all the evidence you'll need, and more, to prosecute this man—this is really none of my business. But may I add something?

"I believe when you receive your copy of this tape, it would be wise to turn it back a few minutes and listen to the man in charge of customer relations tell you the proper board reaction to a crime of this nature committed by a member of your own executive committee. And then, if you have ever respected that man's judgment, respect it now and act upon it."

"How'd they take it?" I asked.

"They were stunned, as you could tell. I'll take some heat for the way I did it, but not from the chairman. He shook my hand warmly before I left and said something about advising 'your Mr. Shipman' to try to keep a straight face, at least until he gets out of the restaurant. Shipper really was having a tough time not cracking up."

"Did you enjoy it, Earl?" Margo asked.

"At first I thought I might. And I still think it was the right thing to do. But, no. Not that he deserved anything better, but it's never pretty to see a man's life disintegrate."

"That's for sure what you were seeing," Bonnie said.

"You said it," Earl agreed.

We sat silent.

"I'm going down the hall to bed," Earl said finally.

I dropped Bonnie off at her apartment and followed Margo home to make sure she got in safely. "I can hardly believe we're finally going to meet Paige," she said as she left the car.

Chapter Eight

Margo and I had agreed to pick up Bonnie on our way to the picnic, but Bonnie called me late in the morning to change plans. "I can hardly believe it," she said, "but Larry just called and asked if he could escort me."

"Larry who?"

"Larry Shipman, of course. What other Larrys do we know?"

"You mean he wants to drive you? It's a little out of his way, isn't it? Why didn't you just tell him we were taking you?"

"I did, but he insisted. He's such a sweet boy. I'm more than old enough to be his mother. In fact, my married daughter is older than he is. But he said he and I would be the fifth and sixth wheels at the park unless we stuck together, so it looks like I have a date."

Margo thought it was neat. "Larry's just being Larry," she said. "Anyway, it'll give us a chance to be alone on the way."

I picked her up around noon, and we carted our picnic paraphernalia north to a forest preserve bordering Highland Park. We were the first ones there.

When Larry came tooling in he leaped from his car and ran around to Bonnie's side before she could get out. He swung the door open and helped her. She laughed and punched him. "Be nice!" he shouted, "or I'll treat you like the grandmother you are."

"You're already treating me like an old lady!"

"You want me to call you 'Mom' right here in public?"

Bonnie was loving it. We sat and chatted about whether we thought Paige could ever live up to her advanced billing. "Don't anyone get the idea that this is really going to be a nonworking day," Bonnie said, pulling her newspaper and several file folders from her huge handbag. "Earl called and asked me to stop by the office and pull the pending files. I imagine he'll be making some assignments today."

None of us really minded. Assignment day is the most fun day of each month for us. Earl talks about each file folder, shows us the photographs and documents and affidavits and leads—anything he's acquired during the initial interviewing stages—then asks for comments. It's like a classroom with the best possible teacher running the show. He asks questions, evaluates our answers, poses hypothetical situations, and challenges us to think. "What's the first thing you'll want to find out?" he'll say. Or, "What are you going to have to watch out for with this client? What if he says this, or what if she does that?"

It is always a stimulating time, and I often realize during my investigations that what Earl predicts is usually right. And when I ask the questions and look under the rocks he suggests, things start to come together.

"I don't suppose you'd let us peek into any of those files and start bidding on cases," Margo suggested.

"You know I can't do that," Bonnie said. "And when was the last time you bought a case?"

"I just hope I proved myself with this welfare thing

70

and that Earl will give me another good one."

"You did," Shipman said. "Earl was impressed. I think he has a lost cat caper in store for you." Margo grabbed Bonnie's paper and swatted him.

"Gimme that," Bonnie said. "I usually don't allow myself out into the light of day without reading my *Tribune*." As she turned to her favorite section, the light of day disappeared and it began to drizzle. We headed toward a small pavilion a few yards from our picnic table.

I was helping lug our stuff and found myself behind Bonnie, who had made an instant tent of the paper and hid her head beneath it. As she spread it out to dry in the pavilion I picked up the soggy first section.

TEEN SUICIDE SHOCKS SKOKIE;
YOUTH LEAVES PUZZLING NOTE

SKOKIE—Police in this north Chicago suburb are questioning friends and relatives of a popular Skokie South High School senior, 18-year-old Brian Lawrence Dahlberg, Jr., who apparently committed suicide at the fashionable family residence here last night.

The youth was found in the garage, behind the wheel of his father's late model car, police say. The engine had been running with the garage door shut, and indications are that the boy's own sports car had been idling in the garage as well.

Ironically, it was the young Dahlberg's father, owner of Dahlberg Industries, Inc., Chicago, who found a six-page letter from his son on the kitchen

71

table, then ran to the garage where he attempted to revive the boy. He has been unavailable for comment.

Speculation among police is that the boy was despondent over the accidental death of a close friend nearly three months ago. They say his letter was "mostly incoherent," and while it has not been released to the press, a police spokesman read the last paragraph, which he said followed three solid pages of "I'm sorry. I'm sorry. I'm sorry."

The final paragraph read: "Sorry doesn't work. I feel no better. I can't forgive myself. It's better I'm gone. Sorry, Dad."

There was more, but I could read no further. I sensed Margo and Larry reading over my shoulder and talking to me, but I didn't respond. My heart raced, and I felt as if I were about to explode. I whirled and looked to where I had parked the car. "Margo," I said, not even looking at her, "can you get a ride home with Larry or Earl?"

"Sure, but Philip—"

I ran to the car and felt the cold October rain flatten my hair and stream down my face. A car pulled in next to mine. I didn't know where I was going, but I had to go. As I started the car Earl shouted at me, and I saw a water-distorted view of him sharing an umbrella with a woman who had just gotten out of his car.

Paige. Earl would understand.

With rain dripping from my hair onto my neck and down my collar, and with tears welling in my eyes, I could hardly see to drive. I went three blocks without turning on my wipers, and I never did think to turn on my lights. I failed to obey a yield sign and heard an angry horn.

Not knowing exactly where I was, and suddenly exhausted, I pulled to the side of a residential street and rested my head against the steering wheel.

"God," I prayed aloud, alarming myself with the tightness of my own voice, "why do I always wait?" I sensed no reply. It was a question without an answer. I could think of nothing else to say. The phrase echoed in my mind, and I sobbed. There is always a reason to wait, always a reason to put it off, always a better time, a better situation, a better place, a better way to bring a person to a higher level of receptivity.

Receptivity. My conversation with Margo the night before haunted me. I had all the answers. While I had been telling her of Brian's "real needs" as opposed to his symptoms, and while I had it all figured out that what he really needed was an anchor in the universe, he was writing his suicide letter.

Margo had asked me why I didn't think he was ready.

The business about how you never know when a person may be hit by a car or die in his sleep had always been a churchy cliche to me. Not only did I now have a friend who was a victim, but I had also had the chance to offer hope. And I had blown it. I had waited.

No one could console me. I didn't need counseling. I was disgusted with myself, and I had a right to be. I hit-and-missed my way back to the Edens Expressway and headed south. I would wait no longer.

All the way to the Keith home, I tried to think of what

to say and how to say it. I prayed for the right words. I knew I was being impulsive and that I might make a fool of myself, but I was also hit again with my question, "Why do I always wait?"

I had heard so many times that if there's anything worth becoming a fool for, it's the salvation of men. If I was about to become a fool for Christ, so be it. I would simply talk to the Keiths about Brian, try to insist that they not take any of the blame—though I knew Mr. Keith would after having hedged on his forgiveness and leaving the boy in despair.

And then I would tell them that I just had to say to them what I had wanted to say to Brian. I would tell them that their wonderful family and their airtight morals and their church attendance were not enough, that if something should happen to them or their daughters as quickly as it had happened to their own son and to Brian Dahlberg, they would need to have received Christ, His love, His pardon, His salvation.

It wouldn't be smooth. They might not understand. The time might not be right. Their receptivity might not be at the best level. But I would not wait. I would not have another experience like the one I had just endured. I didn't want another person I knew to have the chance of being lost simply because I had waited for a better time.

That included Earl, and the Dahlbergs, and Larry, and Bonnie. Margo and I had our priority list, and Earl was right at the top, but I couldn't wait on the others until we got through to Earl. I didn't want to alienate people, and I prayed that I would not do more harm than good or go off half-cocked. I wanted to be sensitive, loving, genuinely concerned. And now when I felt it so deeply, I had an entrée and I would use it.

The Keiths had not seen the paper and were speechless. The man hung his head, and I told him I thought I knew how he felt.

"Do you know that I nearly called him last night to tell him that my wife was right about my reaction?"

I shook my head.

He continued, "And do you know that I wanted to talk with him then? He said we would talk. I said we would talk. I had been horrible to him. I wanted to forgive him, but like you, I waited. You say you had this important message for him, and while I don't understand it and am not sure I even agree with it, I can identify with you. I had a message for him, too. But I waited. I figured I could call him in a few days. I knew my wife would invite him on an outing. I'd get my chance. Only I didn't get it, did I?"

His wife put her arm around his shoulders and patted him. She looked up at me. "We're not really religious like you are, Mr. Spence, but we go to church and try to live right. We'll pray for Brian as we pray for Justin."

I wanted to argue theology with her. I wanted to tell them that all their attempts to do what only God could do would get them nowhere. But I had already said it. They had heard it. They may not have understood it, and they may never. But someday someone will say it again, or they'll read it somewhere, or their pastor will start taking his sermons from Scripture instead of human literature, and the seed I planted will be watered.

"If you have any doubt that you are in right relationship to God, I urge you to seek Him where He can be found, through Christ."

They nodded tolerantly and said they hoped I felt better for telling them, as if I had gotten something off my chest.

Something told me I would no longer be satisfied to just be a sort of Christian hit man, blitzing people with the message and moving on to the next prospect. There was much more to this than just spilling the story and hoping for the best.

On the way to the Dahlberg home I almost found myself debating the timing. If there ever *was* a valid reason for waiting, this might be it. But I couldn't wait. I told Mr. and Mrs. Dahlberg that I was a friend of their son. Then I began with: "There was something I really should have told him last night, and I would give anything to be able to tell him now." They were anxious to hear what it was, and while they responded no more encouragingly than the Keiths, I know they were glad to hear from any friend of Brian's.

My chest felt heavy as I drove to my apartment. I went to bed early and probably would have slept all night and much of Saturday morning. But the phone rang near midnight. It was Margo.

Chapter Nine

"How are you, sweetheart?" she asked.

I sighed deeply and leaned up on one elbow without turning on the lights. "I don't know," I said, thickly. "Just tired."

"Want to talk?"

"I guess."

"Want to meet me somewhere? Are you hungry or anything?"

"No."

"I just want you to know I'm with you," she said.

I couldn't speak. She heard me fighting not to cry again.

"Talk to me, Philip. Then you can go back to sleep."

"Why do we always wait?" I said.

"I don't know."

"Why do we *always* wait? We've always got some reason, some priority, some idea. Can you believe the baloney I was feeding you about this time last night? I sure had all that wisdom confirmed, didn't I?"

"Philip, you can't feel responsible. That boy—"

"Brian."

"Brian had a lot of deep, deep problems."

"I'm not saying I could have prevented his death, Margo. But I had an answer for him. He may not have understood or cared, but he would have had an option."

She didn't say anything. I love that about her. When she speaks, she says the right thing. And when she doesn't speak, it's because that's the best course.

"I learned the same lesson from this, you know," she said finally. "Even though I never knew Brian and couldn't care for him the way you do."

"I hardly knew him myself, Margo. But, yes, I do care for him. Did, anyway."

"Do you want to talk about where you went today?"

I told her about the meetings with both sets of parents. "I'm sorry I left you stranded," I said.

"You didn't. It was sweet that you made sure I could get home before you left. I don't think I would have done that."

"How was the assignment meeting?"

"Earl postponed it. You know he doesn't like to have those without everyone there to put in his two cents' worth. It's scheduled for Monday morning."

"I wonder if Earl will let me talk to the staff for a few minutes."

"Probably. He knows you're upset, and he understands. He wishes you could have met Paige, but he knows you had to leave."

"When will I get to meet her?"

"Sunday afternoon. The rain ruined our picnic, so we're trying again. Same time, same place. We'll have time to change after church and get up there."

"So, tell me about her."

"Wouldn't you rather be sleeping?"

"I *am* sleeping. Tell me about Paige."

"She's really special, Philip. Everything Earl said she was. A selfless, loving person, just the type you'd love to have for a mother or a sister or a nurse or whatever."

"I didn't get a good look at her. What does she look like?"

"She's cute. I know that's a strange description of a forty-year-old woman, but she's cute. Fresh, wholesome, bright. We all just loved her."

"Well, it'll be good to meet her. I'm happy for Earl. So, what are you doing tomorrow?"

"Don't you remember? That's why I called you tonight, because I'm leaving early in the morning to spend the day in Milwaukee with Bonnie. One of her kids lives there, and we were going to just blow the whole day. I'll cancel if you want and stay with you. Bonnie will understand."

"No way, hon. You've been looking forward to this."

"Well, why don't you go with us? It'll get your mind off Brian a little."

"Nah. That's not my idea of a diversion. You guys enjoy yourselves. I need a good day with nothing to do. If I get bored I may talk Earl and Ship into going downtown or something."

"You won't be talking Earl into anything. You can bet he'll be with Paige every waking moment."

"Right. Anyway, have a good time, don't worry about

me, and I'll pick you up Sunday morning at nine."

"I love you, Philip."

"Of course you do. You can't help yourself."

"Oh, shut up. At least you still have your sense of humor."

"Yeah, and isn't that wonderful?" I said, wryly. "Sometimes we Christians bounce back so quickly it's disgusting."

"Don't be too hard on yourself."

"I won't. I'm just tired. I'll see ya."

I slept until nearly noon on Saturday, then went out for lunch, deciding to walk about a mile and a half to a greasy spoon. My trench coat felt baggy, though warm against a shivery breeze, and I spent a couple of blocks trying to decide why. The answer was at the edge of consciousness, and I worked at trying to keep it there. It was an idle, stupid exercise, something I have often done. As the obvious answer took shape, I tried to think of other things, scolding myself for playing grade-school games as the truth forced its way into my head: *Your trenchcoat is baggier than usual because you're not wearing a suit coat like you usually do.*

Silliness. I used to like being alone. Now I was weird alone. I needed a wife. I needed Margo.

I hadn't completely dried my hair after my shower, and the wind made me shudder. *Grief,* I thought, *I need more than a wife; I need a mother!*

I pulled my collar up around my neck and thrust my hands deep into the pockets of my coat. *Why am I* walking so fast? I asked myself. *Nothing to do today, no obligations*. I slowed and then deliberately veered off the sidewalk to walk through some leaves.

But they weren't dry and crackly. They'd been rained on and were merely mushy and muddy. I still liked the odor. Sweet. Not yet moldy with death, but dead just the same. And from death, life. The greatest truth of my faith.

My leather heels clicked on the pavement as I crossed a street and entered the Hole-in-the-Wall, a most appropriately named hash house. I ordered a Polish sausage and a Coke.

I ate slowly, trying to push everything from my mind. But as the food and drink worked their magic on my system, I began to eat faster. It suddenly became important to get finished, to head back, to call Larry, to do something, anything. I wasn't going to vegetate. I couldn't just sit around. I had to do something, even if it wasn't productive—a mutation of the Protestant Work Ethic, married to the Now and the Me generations. Do something, have fun, experience, whatever.

I walked briskly back to my apartment, ignoring the sights and sounds and smells I had enjoyed on the way. I played no more silly mind games. Earl's car was gone. He would be with Paige. What was Larry's home number? I looked it up in the office and called him from there.

"Hey, Philip, glad you called! Margo's gone with Bonnie, huh? I just had a guy stiff me who was gonna drive into Indiana with me today, so I'm looking for something to do. Whatcha got in mind?"

"Oh, I don't care. Anything. I'd be happy to drive to your place if there's anything going on around there. Hold on a second, Ship, there's a call coming in."

"We don't answer on Saturdays," Shipman said.

"No, I'd better take it. Hang on." I never have been good at ignoring ringing phones or doorbells. It was Earl.

"I've been trying to reach you at home," he said. "Glad I caught you. You OK?"

"Sure, thanks. I want to talk to you about it sometime, Earl, but for now, yeah, I'm all right. I've got Larry on the other line. What can I do for you?"

"Oh, good. I wanted him too. Listen, is there any chance you two could come to the rehab center today? I don't want to tell you what it's all about yet, but I need your help. Anyway, it'll give you a chance to meet Paige."

"No problem for me, Earl. I'm free. Let me ask Larry. Hold on."

"The rehab center is about midway between us," Larry told me. "If we each leave within the next fifteen minutes, we can meet there in forty-five. See you there."

At least there'd be something interesting happening today, even if it was simply getting to meet Paige.

When I pulled into the parking lot at the institution, Larry and Paige were waiting with Earl in his car. I slid into the backseat with Larry, directly behind Paige. She turned around and smiled. What a doll. She reached back and took my hand as Earl introduced us. "I've heard so much about you," she said. "And your fiancee is a lovely girl. You must be very proud."

I told her I had heard a lot about her too, was glad to meet her, and all that, but I was nearly speechless otherwise. Had it been the middle of the night, Earl wouldn't have needed his headlights. She glowed, just as everyone had said. I wanted to ask Earl what he wanted, but he and Larry were already involved in conversation. Paige turned completely around in her seat and leaned over the back to whisper to me.

"Philip," she said, "I was horrified to hear about your young friend, and I want you to know that if there's anything I can do, or if you want to talk about it—or even if you *don't* want to talk about it, just let me know."

"I appreciate that, Mrs. Holiday. And I think I don't want to talk about it for a while."

"I understand," she said. "These things can be traumatic. Well, then, tell me about yourself and where you're from. Margo already told me about your unusual meeting and courtship, but I know very little about your background."

I told her about my home in Dayton, Ohio, and that I had always wanted to be a free-lance artist until I got involved with Earl. "He's quite a guy," I said. She smiled and crinkled her nose.

I tried to get her to talk about herself, but she just told me what Earl had said, that she was a widow and had lost her only child at birth. "And you're from—?"

"Saint Paul," she said. "Been there?"

"Nope."

"You'd love it. Did Earl tell you that there's been some encouragement with Earl, Jr.?"

"No! Earl," I interrupted, "what's this?"

"Paige says he seems to be responding to her, mostly when no other children or adults are around. He might have smiled and once even tried to talk."

Paige nodded.

"Incredible!" I said. "That's unusual after this long, isn't it? I mean, he's how old now?"

"Thirteen," Earl said.

"Has he responded to you, Earl?"

"Not yet. I can't really see any difference, but it's all I can think about right now."

"That's a switch," Larry said, winking at Paige. She tried to suppress a smile and stole a glance at Earl.

"We'll talk later," she said, looking deep into my eyes and turning back to the front seat. "OK?"

"Sure," I said. Neat lady.

Earl pulled into a posh restaurant. "Oh, no," I said.

"Have no fear, gentlemen," he said. "This one's on me."

"I'd love to help you celebrate this progress with Little Earl," I said, "but I just ate."

"That's all right, Philip," Paige said. "You can watch us eat."

· "Anyway," Earl said, holding the door for everyone, "we're not here to celebrate, although that's not a bad idea. I just may have a new case."

"A new case?"

"Let's order, and then I'll tell you about it."

As we looked at the menus, Paige asked Larry about his career as a stringer for the local papers and broadcast media, obviously picking up where they had left off at the aborted picnic the day before. She really had a way of bringing out the best in people. She could talk to men in front of Earl without flirting or ignoring him. In fact, she had a way of including him, even when he wasn't really part of the conversation.

I didn't know how far their relationship had progressed, whether he had even told her of his affection for her, but it was obvious that she cared for him. She cared for everybody, but I sensed that she even knew what he was thinking. Her inner beauty, which manifested itself in her expressive face, was even more amazing to me when I learned a few minutes later that our next case would revolve around her.

I never would have guessed anything was out of kilter in her life, the way she had given herself to conversation and to the group. I could tell why Earl was so taken with her, and why he would ask us to join him to start the investigation—or whatever was necessary—with all the heads available.

"I'm going to tape this so Bonnie and Margo can know what you boys know," Earl explained. "I want all the help I can get."

Chapter Ten

"Do you want to tell the story, Paige?" Earl asked.

"No, you go ahead. You know at least as much of it as I do."

"When I took Paige back to the rehab center after the picnic yesterday, there was a note from her supervisor that she was to report immediately. I waited around, since she was not really on duty anyway and we were planning to go out.

"When Paige returned from her meeting, I could tell she was troubled. I had never seen her show even a trace of fatigue or frustration or depression before."

I knew what he meant. I couldn't imagine Paige looking troubled. Even now, she was simply listening to him the way she listens to everyone.

"It took a long time for me to drag it out of her, but it seems a young girl, sixteen or seventeen, showed up at the center Friday and demanded to see Paige Datilo. The supervisor told her the only Paige on the staff was Paige Holiday.

" 'That's her,' the girl supposedly said. 'Holiday was her maiden name. Unless she's remarried, her name is

Datilo, just like mine. Tell Paige Datilo her daughter was here.' "

Shipman and I looked at each other, and then at Paige and Earl. "So, what's the truth?" Shipman asked, as if it were the most obvious and logical question he could think of. "What *is* your maiden name, Mrs. Holiday?"

"Nothing ethnic, that's for sure," she said. "Just Greene with an *e*, that's all."

"Can you prove that?" Larry said.

Paige did a double take, and Earl scowled. "Sorry," Larry said. "Just askin'."

"Somehow the interviewing techniques I admire so much in you don't seem to be called for here," Earl said coldly.

"Are you sure you can be objective about this one, Earl?" Ship asked.

"Absolutely."

The way he said it proved him wrong, but he was too close to see it. "And if you want to try interrogating someone, why don't you start by tracking down this little opportunist and finding out who she is?"

"Where do we start?" Larry asked.

"Three guesses," Earl said. "Really, Larry, you want me to tell you where to start looking for someone?"

"I suppose I should start with the only woman we know of who has seen her."

"I suppose," Earl said, condescendingly. Paige touched Earl's arm and spoke his name quietly. It seemed to transform him. "I'm sorry, Ship," he said. "But you're one of the best in the business. You don't need to ask, 'Where do I start?' do you?"

"Of course not, Earl, and forgive me, Mrs. Holiday. I shouldn't have sounded accusatory."

She flashed that warming smile and assured him it was OK. "My supervisor's name is Marilyn Fleagle. She works Tuesdays through Saturdays until six."

"Then she's still there," I said, looking at my watch.

"Oh, both you guys are up for gold stars," Earl said, still frustrated with Larry but pretending to be kidding.

"I'm not eating," I said. "Why don't I just head over there?"

"Because we have only one car here, dummy," Earl said, smiling. I smacked myself on the forehead with an open palm. Larry laughed. Paige looked sympathetic. I wanted to hug her. An hour later, we all sat in Mrs. Fleagle's office.

"Mr. Haymeyer, I already answered your questions. Must we take more time?"

"If you don't mind," Earl said, "I would appreciate it if you would fill in my colleagues. Mr. Shipman here will be handling the case."

"The case? What case? Mrs. Holiday's or Datilo's daughter comes in here to see her and you call it a case?"

"We'll be investigating it."

"Investigating it? Now it's more than a case. It's an investigation. What *is* all this?"

Shipman answered. "You don't think this girl was lying?"

"No. Why should she lie? She looked a little like Mrs. Holiday."

"In what way?"

"As I told Mr. Haymeyer," she said, shifting her mass in the high-backed chair and scowling under a full head of white hair, "she had those even teeth that Mrs. Holiday has. Her coloring was much darker, and her hair was jet black. But she was built small, and there was a resemblance."

Paige had said nothing. "Doesn't it bother you, Paige, that your boss thinks this girl could have been telling the truth when you say there's nothing to it?" I asked.

Paige smiled knowingly at Mrs. Fleagle. "Not really," she said. "Our disagreements go back about six weeks when I first joined the staff. I didn't have the experience she wanted, but I was good with the children and she needed someone."

"That's not quite all of it, is it, Mrs. *Holiday?*" the old woman said, putting sarcasm into the name as if certain Paige was hiding behind it.

"I don't know what you mean," Paige said, still unruffled and looking the woman right in the eye.

"I mean that this is not the first time I have caught you in a lie."

Earl reddened. "Surely you don't mean you have caught Paige in a lie," he said. "You may have disagreed about something, but why wouldn't you fire a person you think has lied to you?"

"As Mrs. *Holiday* herself just said, I needed someone. People who deal with this type of handicapped children are not easy to find." The woman immediately softened as she remembered that Earl was more than a detective; he was also a father. "I'm sure you know what I mean," she said carefully.

"Yes, I do," Earl said. "And I've never seen anyone deal with autistic children the way Paige does."

"There's more to dealing with them than smiling at them," Mrs. Fleagle said.

"Good grief, what are you saying?" Earl said. "Is there something wrong with a woman trying to draw out an autistic child with a beautiful smile?"

"Of course not. It's just that she doesn't draw them out. She just says she does."

"Could we rephrase that?" Paige suggested. "I'd rather think that if I am wrong, I am simply mistaken. I don't just say that I've drawn a response. I truly believe that I have. Only you or someone else more qualified would know for sure. But you haven't been present when the children have smiled at me or tried to communicate."

"Indeed I have not. And in fact no one else has been around, have they?"

Paige seemed to smile forgivingly at the old woman. It was as if she had thought of just the right sarcastic remark to put Mrs. Fleagle in her place, but Paige held her tongue. I was proud of her. And nearly as defensive of her as Earl was.

"Earl," Shipman said, "I wonder if Mr. Spence and I could talk with Mrs. Fleagle alone for a few minutes. It's obvious there is tension between these women, and you have two reasons to have a vested interest in this. What do you say?"

Earl started to argue, but Paige nodded to him.

"I did say you would be handling it," Earl said. "We'll be outside."

When just the three of us were left in the room, Shipman turned on his boyish charm. "Please forgive Mr. Haymeyer," he said. "He's a professional like you are, but I'm afraid with his son having been here since he was a toddler, and with his obvious affection for Mrs. Holiday, whom he barely knows, he is a little defensive."

"Oh, that's quite all right," Mrs. Fleagle said. "I understand."

"May I call you Marilyn?" Shipman asked.

She was ready to say no, I'm sure, but when she raised her eyes to glare at him, she had to return his huge grin. "I suppose," she said hesitantly, "as long as you don't insist that I call you Larry or Shippy or whatever it is they call you."

She hadn't meant it to be funny, but Larry threw his head back and laughed loudly. "Well, they call me a lot of things, Marilyn, but Shippy isn't one of them. You can call me anything you like, as long as it's clean, know what I mean?"

A smile invaded her face. "I prefer to call you Mr. Shipman, if you don't mind."

"Not at all. Now, Marilyn, the first thing I want to know is if we have already overstayed our welcome"—she looked as if she had been waiting for a chance to graciously get rid of us—"because if we have, I want you to feel perfectly free to just tell us and name the date and time so we can reschedule. It's no problem for us to cancel other appointments and coordinate our calendars and make the trip down here. You just tell us."

"Well, how much more time did you want?"

"Just a few minutes, ma'am."

"Then I'd just as soon finish this tonight. I can stay a little later to finish my work if I have to. Clarence is working late tonight himself."

"Your husband? I'd love to meet him some day."

"No, you wouldn't," she said, laughing. "I've been waiting years to say that!"

Shipman realized she considered that funny, and he roared a little too late and a little flatly, but she didn't notice. He had her now.

"Why do you think Mrs. Holiday is using her maiden name and doesn't want to see her daughter, Marilyn?"

"Oh, I didn't say that."

"But you think it, don't you? I mean, you really tend to believe the girl more than your employee for some reason."

"Yes, I suppose I do."

"Why? Is it because Paige is naive? Because she comes in here with no training and thinks she's reaching the unreachable?"

"That's not totally it, Larry, uh, Mr. Shipman. But I suppose it's part of it. At first I liked it. Anybody would. She's a beautiful woman, that smile of hers and all. And she does seem to care for the children. But she's not reaching them any more than I reached them when I had her job for more than twenty years. You love those children until it hurts; you give them everything you have to give. You try every new technique and therapy that comes along, and only a handful out of the hundreds ever seems to make any progress."

"I understand, Marilyn. So it bothers you when she is optimistic."

"I would never begrudge anyone optimism. The point is that she lies."

"But she admits she could be wrong, and she says you would know."

"It's not a matter of being wrong. She lies."

"Those are pretty strong words," I interrupted, feeling Shipman's stare because I had stepped on his choreographed system of drawing her out. Now I had offended her.

"Perhaps they are," she said. "But I have caught her in lies."

"Actual lies?" Larry said, raising a hand to keep me out of the conversation.

"Actual lies."

"She admits them, when she's caught?"

"No, and that's what bothers me. I've had any number of employees who tell little white lies to stay out of hot water. If they lose something, they say they never saw it. If they break something when no one's around, they deny it. But when they are caught red-handed, they just apologize. It's human nature. But this woman never admits her wrongdoing. I'm telling you that if I were to believe this woman, I would have to think she was nearly perfect. And now I'm supposed to believe that she's getting through to some of the toughest cases we have? No, sir."

"Marilyn," Larry said softly. "I think you know people, and I'm not trying to patronize you." He hesitated, and they smiled at each other as if both knew he was full of hot air. "But I want you to tell me everything you can about this young girl. I want to find her and talk to her, and you have my assurance that if she *is* Mrs. Holiday's daughter, we will report back to you and see that this situation is rectified."

"I might as well tell you, and you can tell Mrs. Holiday," she said, "that any major shenanigan like this will not be tolerated. If she's lying about this, she's gone, short of staff or not."

"I understand, Marilyn," Shipman said, "and thank you very much."

Chapter Eleven

Somehow, Larry talked Mrs. Fleagle into letting me make copies of everything in Paige's personnel file. I made two so Larry could take a set home.

He filled in Earl and said he was confident we could clear the thing up. When Earl took Paige home, Larry and I lingered in the parking lot to chat.

"The supervisor bothers me as much as she does everyone else," he admitted. "But I don't think we're going to get anything out of her by putting her on the defensive. Anyway, now that she's given us Paige's files, she really doesn't figure into the case anymore. Unless the girl shows up here again."

"I disagree," I said. "I think this woman has it in for Paige somehow. She could be making up this whole story. Even so, it would be nice if in the course of the investigation, we could make things smoother for Paige to work here. It can't be any fun when your supervisor doesn't trust you."

"True enough, but Paige seems like she can hold her own and make the best of any situation. I think she derives her pleasure and fulfillment from working with the kids."

"I'm anxious to get into her file and see her background," I said. "There's something special about her."

"How many do you know?"

"Who are like she is, you mean?"

"Yeah."

"Not many."

"That's what I thought. See you at the picnic tomorrow, and don't bring any business."

"I won't if you won't," I said.

Paige's file reflected everything she had told us. "Maiden name: Greene. Last previous residence: 314 Main St., St. Paul, MN. Marital status: widow. Children: None—lost unnamed male in childbirth, 1969."

Her forms showed six years of nurses' aide experience, followed by eight years of public school teaching in the largest elementary school district in St. Paul. She had moved to the Chicago area when her forte, special education, was phased out of the public school system and put under another state department. She wrote on the application that she could have taken a job with the state in a similar capacity, but since her husband had died the previous summer, she decided to simply start over in another city.

I admired her. She was self-confident, sure, but even the most aggressive people are hesitant to pull up stakes at age forty and start over. I wanted to take the file with me to the picnic Sunday and talk to Larry about it, but I had promised. I would, however, have it in the car so

Margo could see it and so I could tell her all about what had happened.

She called at about eleven to tell me she and Bonnie had returned safely. "I'm almost too exhausted to think about church tomorrow," she said. I think she was waiting for me to tell her not to worry about it, so I didn't say anything. "But, I guess I'll try to make it, at least for the worship service at eleven," she said.

"Well, I was going to tell you about a big new case we're all going to get involved in, but I suppose it can wait until later."

"See you at nine sharp," she said.

I fell asleep with Paige's file all over the bed.

There was hardly time to tell Margo everything during the short ride to church the next morning, so she insisted on taking the file inside with her and peeking at it while we waited for the service to begin. I kept making faces at her, but she was fascinated.

"What do you suppose this Fleagle woman's problem is?" she asked.

I shrugged.

On the way back to Margo's apartment, where I would wait in the car for her to change and get a picnic basket ready, she told me to read the miscellaneous memos attached to Paige's file. I thought I had seen everything of any relevance, but I agreed.

"I'll be right back," she said, bounding up the stairs. I opened the folder again and dug out the notes that had passed between Mrs. Fleagle and her boss, who was

99

known in the file only as J.T. She gave J.T. a glowing recommendation on Paige and suggested that she be hired, even though it was proving difficult for the personnel department to track down the references Paige listed. "All have changed jobs, moved, or died within the last eight months," she noted.

"References are not as crucial at this level as they might be at another," J.T. had replied. "If you are confident of her potential, proceed."

"You think that's relevant?" I asked as Margo returned.

"I don't know, but it is a loose end. The kind Earl always catches."

"He wouldn't have caught this loose end. It's a chink in Paige's armor."

"Oh, it is not. It's not her fault her references are hard to locate. And Earl would too have found it. He's sharper than that."

"Not when it comes to Paige, believe me."

"I'm going to ask him at the picnic."

"C'mon, let's not talk business there. I promised Larry I wouldn't even bring the file."

Now it was Margo's turn to wait in the car while I changed. On the way north to the forest preserve, she read the entire file again. "Sure doesn't appear that she could have had any connection with anyone named Datilo, or that she has a daughter anywhere. Even the child she lost was a boy."

"Where does it say she went to college?" I asked.

"University of Minnesota. Why?"

"Just curious. Should be easy enough to corroborate all her information."

"Why do you suppose she took such a low-paying job here, compared to what she had before?" Margo said.

"Ever try to get a teaching job without local tenure? She probably took this job so she could eat, and then liked it so much she wanted to stay."

"I don't imagine she's had any time to look for other work, now that she's been seeing Earl," Margo said. "It's too bad this supervisor has it in for her. It would be a tragedy for the kids if they lost a friend like Paige."

When we arrived at the picnic it was obvious before we got out of the car that I needn't feel guilty about bringing the file. Larry had his out and was reading it to Bonnie. Earl and Paige were peering over their shoulders.

"You turkey," I shouted, "I thought you weren't going to bring work!"

Everyone looked up and smiled, except Shipman. "This is all I needed to see," Earl said. "You guys did the job. I'm just curious about the young girl now, and I want to know what her scheme is. What do you think? Does she want money? A free ride? What?"

"Does she sound like anyone you have ever known, Paige?" Margo said. "A relative, an old acquaintance?"

Paige thought and shook her head.

"Hold it!" Bonnie said. "That's enough business. Earl, if you don't put a stop to this and get on with the picnic, I'm leaving. I love this work just as much as the rest of you, but we've got to put it behind us for one day and relax."

"This isn't business," Earl said, a little too curtly. "It's Paige."

Bonnie flushed. "I'm sorry, Earl. I know you're worried about it."

"Worried? Naw. Why should I be worried? It's probably just some local high school kids pulling a prank. Let's have a picnic!"

When we started breaking out the goodies, I overheard Earl tell Paige and Bonnie, "I'm not going to even let it enter my mind any more today. Why waste time on trivia?"

Later, while we were tossing a football around, he told Ship, "You guys'll have this thing wrapped up quick, and we won't even have to bother with it any more. It's silly. Not worth even talking about."

As we were leaving, Earl put his arm around me. "Hey, don't worry about this thing with Paige. I've put it out of my mind. No sense letting it get in the way of business. You guys give it another day or so and get a bead on this kid and meanwhile, I won't even think about it."

I just looked at him. He was spending so much time not thinking about it that it was running his life. Even Paige looked a little tense, but as usual, she put everyone else's needs before her own. She was the one who pitched in first for serving and cleaning up and running errands. Earl was a lucky guy. Now if she could just get him to *really* forget about her phantom high school tormentor and the boss who had cooled on her so quickly.

"Have you thought about the possibility that Mrs. Fleagle might have fabricated this whole thing?" Margo ventured. I saw Larry give her the quiet sign from behind Earl's back and shake his head. But it was too late.

"I have," Earl said, putting his foot up on our bumper and warming to the subject. "Has she given you reason to think she might do something like that, Paige?" he asked.

"I hadn't thought of it," she said. "I doubt it. Behind that crusty exterior is a woman who is really a professional. Even though I fear she has me misjudged, I don't think I could accuse her of making up stories to hurt me."

"Well, that's just the way you are, Paige," Earl said. "I think you may be right, Margo. Let's talk about it at our meeting in the morning. Meanwhile, I'm putting the whole thing out of my mind." This time no one reacted. And no one smiled. Earl was becoming obsessed.

Just before Earl and Paige pulled out of the parking lot, I jogged up to his door. "Earl, would it be all right if I spoke to the staff for a few minutes tomorrow morning?"

"What about?"

"Well, it's just that everyone knew about the case I was working on with the Keith boy, and that his friend Brian killed himself. I just want to bring everyone up to date, you know."

"Yeah. You're not going to get religious on us now, are you?"

"No guarantees, Earl. I promise not to take more than

ten or fifteen minutes if you will agree not to put any restrictions on what I can talk about."

"Now Philip," Earl said, "we've been through this before, and many of us even know what you're trying to pitch. I just think—"

"Earl, you have no idea how important this is to me. I want to tell you guys what I wish I'd been able to tell Brian Dahlberg."·

Earl pursed his lips. "If I let you do this, will you agree not to pressure anyone or keep after them if they don't want to talk any more about it?"

"Sure, but what if they do?"

"They won't, but that's up to them. All right. Ten minutes. You can have the first ten in the assignment meeting, then it's all business. Fair enough?"

"Fair enough. And thanks, Earl."

"Yeah, yeah," he said, driving off.

I skipped back to my car, jumped in, and embraced Margo, planting a huge kiss.

"What's this?" she managed. "You get a raise or something?"

"He said yes!"

"Yes what?"

"Yes I can talk to the staff tomorrow for ten minutes."

"That's not enough time, Philip," she said, suddenly serious.

"It is for me," I said.

"Slow down, Billy Sunday. You're gonna have to really plan and pray."

"Mostly pray, I think."

104

"That's more like it. You want any help?"

"You bet. Anything you've got."

"All I have is encouragement, but I have a lot of that. Let's drive down to the beach, and you can start planning how you're gonna use your ten minutes."

"It really doesn't sound like much, does it?"

"No. But it is. It's ten minutes more than you ever had before," she said.

"I think maybe we'd better go to church tonight and go to the beach after that."

Margo smiled.

Chapter Twelve

On our way out to the car from church that night, Larry Shipman met us in the parking lot. "I'm glad I caught you," he said. "I had no idea how long these rallies lasted."

"You mean church services?" Margo asked.

"Whatever. Anyway, what are the possibilities you two could spend some time with me right now?"

"Well, we did have a date at the lakefront," I said. "What's up?"

"It's this thing with Paige. I think we've all got our heads in the sand over it, and I want Margo to hear the original tape of our dinner conversation and look again at Paige's personnel folder."

"I'd like to hear it," Margo said, "if you think it's necessary. There'll still be time to go to the lakefront, Philip."

"What I want to do," Larry said, "if you don't mind, is to have us listen to the tape at your apartment, Philip, since it's so close. I'd rather not be listening to the tape in the office when Earl gets back from Paige's place."

"Why not?" I said. "He wanted Margo to hear it, didn't he?"

"Yes, but frankly I think we're going to come to different conclusions than Earl, and we won't know what to say when he walks in if we've just been discussing how to properly investigate this thing without his interference."

"Without his *interference*?" Margo said. "Yes, Larry, I think we'd better talk."

We tossed our coats across the bed and stretched out on the floor to hear the tape. "I don't want to prejudice you any more than I already have," he said, "but listen carefully. You were there, Philip, but maybe hearing it again will give you something new. Margo, tell me what you hear."

Nothing hit me. It was just Earl telling the story of the young girl who had claimed to be Paige's daughter. I shrugged as the tape ended.

"So, what did you hear, Margo?" Shipman asked.

"You mean beyond what you guys had already told me?"

"I mean what did you hear with your heart?"

"Ship," I said with a snicker, "you sound like a B-movie."

"Just listen," he said, rewinding the tape and starting it again. I went to the kitchen and made some popcorn. I didn't care how many times I heard it, I didn't know what Larry was driving at. He was going to have to tell me.

I brought in a big bowl and then started pouring Cokes. Margo said, "When I listen emotionally—that's what you're getting at, isn't it, Larry?—" he nodded

"—I hear nothing but Earl."

"Right!"

"Of course she hears Earl," I said, frustrated. "Earl told the story!"

"But I hear more than the story, Philip," she said. "I hear Earl's love of Paige getting in the way of his reason."

"He's been that way since he first met her," I countered. "So what else is new?"

"It hasn't affected his work that much," Larry said. "He's been dreamy about her, but you said yourself that when he talked business he was right on the money. He's nowhere near precise on this one. And he doesn't really want us to check it out. He wants us to bury it."

"Do you know something we don't know?"

"No, and I wouldn't accuse Earl of that, either. It's just that he can't fathom Paige with any dark corners in her past."

"I can't either," I admitted.

"Nor I," Margo said.

"Well, none of us can, don't you see?" Larry said. "That's why we're all breathing collective sighs of relief when we read her personnel file."

"It *does* document what she says," Margo offered.

"No, it doesn't. We want her to be telling the truth so badly that we use her records to corroborate her testimony, a cardinal sin of evidence gathering. Who do you think filled out the lousy personnel forms?"

Margo and I looked at each other. "Paige, of course."

"Of course. Now here, look at the file again."

We ignored our snacks and bent over Ship as he spread the documents on the floor. "Her maiden name was Greene. There are probably a ton of those in the Twin Cities. And, if we're going to be picky, catch this address: Main Street. How many of those do you suppose might be in Saint Paul?"

"Excuse me, Larry," Margo said, "but why do we want to suspect Paige's personnel file? This stuff should be easy enough to check."

"You're right, but Earl may not want us digging into her past, not because he suspects anything, but because he *doesn't* suspect anything."

"I don't follow," I said.

"He's so sure that she's the tormented victim here that he doesn't want to insult her by checking up on her. In fact, he doesn't want *us* insulting *him* by checking up on her."

"So you're saying," Margo decided, "that we should routinely check her background, just as we would any new client, because so often the client doesn't tell us the whole story."

"Exactly."

"And you're convinced that Earl won't see the logic in this?"

"Want to hear the tape again, girl?" Larry asked.

"No."

"Or do you just want to think back to the picnic today and the number of times Earl put the whole thing completely out of his mind?"

Margo and I looked at each other and smiled. "So,

how we gonna pull this off, Ship?" I said.

"I want you to check it out," he said. "You may have to go to Minnesota."

"I'm going to Minnesota without Earl knowing? No way. He's not blind."

"I can handle it," Shipman said. "Maybe I can arrange to trace the girl to Minnesota, and you would go there to track her."

"You mean deceive Earl? I couldn't."

"Then let me. Philip, you have to realize how important this is. We'll find a logical reason for you to go north, and while you're there, confirm the information Paige put in her personnel file. That's all."

"OK, Ship," I said. "If you can find me a legitimate reason to go. Otherwise, no."

Margo and I spent an hour and a half in the car at the Lake Michigan waterfront around midnight, praying and planning what I would say the next morning. We needn't have bothered. Earl met me as I came in the office door at 8:00 A.M.

"Philip," he said, "I'm not the type to back out on a promise—you know that. But I'm going to have to ask you to postpone your little talk. More has come up in this case with Paige, and we need the time to hash it out. I guarantee you I'll reschedule it, and you'll get up to a half hour, no restrictions, OK?"

I was really disappointed, but I had no choice. I couldn't hold my boss to his promise, and he *had* made a major concession. Just before the assignment meeting I spoke quietly with Margo.

"I feel like I'm waiting again," I said. "And I determined never to wait again."

"You can't control this situation, babe," she said. "Be glad he gave you more time. You'll be able to explain it all clearly, without fear of slipping into cliches and sounding religious—"

"Which seems to be Earl's biggest fear."

"Right. Let's take this as if it was meant to be and make the most of it."

When we were all assembled, Earl began. "I'm asking Bonnie to contact all our clients whose cases are in the pending file to tell them we'll be getting to them as soon as possible. There are several interesting ones there, and I'm sure you will each be pleased at your assignments. But for now, I want this business with Paige cleared away."

"But you said yesterday that Philip and I should just give it a few more days and be done with it."

"I know that, Ship," Earl said. "If you'll just let me continue. Paige called early this morning and said one of the neighbors in her apartment complex told her a young girl had been nosing around, asking questions and claiming to be Paige's daughter. It's really starting to get to her, and I'd like us to concentrate on finding this girl fast. I want to know what her angle is so we can put Paige's mind at ease."

"Do we have a lead on the neighbor?" Larry asked. "It would be good to have someone talk to her."

"You can check that out with Paige. I also want someone to talk with Mrs. Fleagle again. She doesn't

112

work Mondays, but you should be able to locate her. I want to know if she noticed whether the girl appeared to have been traveling, or was local, or what."

"You still want me to handle this?" Shipman asked.

"Yes, I do."

"Then may I make a suggestion? I think you should simply observe and make recommendations. I really feel you're too close to this to be making judgments and decisions. I probably should have told you that in private, but I feel it's important."

"Forgive me for speaking up," Bonnie said. "I'm not supposed to speak in these meetings, I know, but I think Larry is right. Earl, you owe it to yourself and to Paige to stay out of this investigation."

Earl was hot. There's no way around it. I thought he was going to blow and tell us that he could handle the pressure and remain objective. But he didn't. "I suppose you're right," he said, not sounding totally convinced. "I want to spend a lot of time with Paige until this is over anyway, so I don't suppose I'd be too valuable. What's your first move?"

"Is Paige working today?"

"Yup."

"I want Margo to go with you to see her on her break. Get the whole picture of what her neighbor told her. Meanwhile, Philip can talk to Paige briefly and then track down the neighbor to get her complete statement. I'll go to the administrative office and see if I can get Marilyn's address or phone number."

"Marilyn?" Earl said. "Who's Marilyn?"

"Mrs. Fleagle."

"Somehow she doesn't hit me as a Marilyn," Earl said, shaking his head.

"Let's get going," Larry said. "We'll meet in my car in the parking lot at ten thirty this morning to report."

I started my search at the rehab center, calling Paige away from her job for a minute to get the name and address of her neighbor. "I don't even know her name," she said. "She lives a floor above me and she works. Lives alone, I think. I'm sorry I can't be more help. She came by to tell me this morning on her way to work."

"But you don't know where she works or anything?"

"No."

"What does she look like?"

"Oh, average build. Middle-aged. Brown hair. Plain."

"Great."

"I know I haven't been of much help, Philip. And I'm sorry."

"That's OK. If that girl was nosing around, I'm sure someone else saw her too. Wish me luck."

She flashed me an appreciative smile and gave me a thumbs-up sign. "Oh, I almost forgot," she said. "Will you tell Earl something for me?"

"You can tell him yourself in a few minutes. He and Margo are coming to see you."

"Oh, good, because Mrs. Fleagle came by today and threatened to make trouble for me if I didn't shape up."

"Make trouble for you? How?"

"She didn't say."

"And how are you supposed to shape up?"

"I don't know, Philip. I wish I did. I guess if I'd admit to some rules infraction or something, she'd like me more."

On my way out I saw Ship and Earl and Margo in the waiting room. "She help you much?" Earl asked.

"Not really. Good thing I'm good at this."

Everyone smiled.

At Paige's apartment building I talked to everyone at home on six floors, and none of them had seen a teenage girl they hadn't recognized. Most knew Paige, the new tenant with the lovely smile, but no one on Paige's floor or on the ones immediately above and below hers fit the description of the plain, average, brown-haired, middle-aged, single working woman, and no one knew of her, either.

It was nearly ten thirty, and I had little to report but my puzzlement.

Chapter Thirteen

"What've you got?" Shipman asked me as I got into the car. Earl and I were in the backseat, Margo on the passenger's side in the front next to Larry.

"Not a thing," I said. "Whoever that woman was, she's disappeared or never existed."

"What do you mean by that?" Earl demanded. "Are you saying Paige dreamed this up?"

"I'm saying, Earl," I said coldly, "that no one else saw the girl, no one recognizes the woman by Paige's description, and no one there looked like her. Paige doesn't know her name, describes her as plain and average and alone and a working woman. No, I'm not saying she dreamed her up. I'm just saying I had a frustrating morning and this thing is starting to appear pretty strange."

"Well, just be careful about ascribing to Paige any—"

Larry interrupted. "I'm sorry, boss, but this *is* starting to stink. I gotta tell ya, Paige may not be coming clean with us."

"What are you talking about?" Earl said.

"C'mon, Earl!" Larry said, exasperated. "I think

117

we're all just a little tired of your defensiveness. Paige is a wonderful gal, and we're all impressed with her—though admittedly not in love with her—but we're checking this thing out just the way we check everything, and we're turning up some disconcerting information. Are we not allowed to double-check any of it, or should we just sweep the whole thing under the rug?"

"There's nothing to hide. But you'd better tell me what you mean by the fact that Paige may not be coming clean with you."

"You don't want to know what I've got."

"Of course I do."

"Look at this."

Larry held out a handwritten note penned in a heavy back-slanted style that read, "Dear Peggy: You have until exactly noon on Tuesday to get out of my life. Otherwise, I make no guarantees."

It was signed, "Your former mother."

"So what?" Earl said. "What is it, where'd it come from? Who wrote it?"

"Mrs. Fleagle said Paige brought it by her house this morning and demanded that she give it to the woman at the reception desk inside and instruct her to give it to the teen girl if she showed up again. Here's the envelope."

It read: "Peggy Datilo."

Haymeyer swore. "That's ridiculous," he said, "And Margo will tell you why."

"It does look like Mrs. Fleagle is doing just what Paige claimed she would do," Margo said. "She told us this morning that Mrs. Fleagle threatened to pull something like this."

"She said something to me like that this morning too," I said, "but I thought she said yesterday that she didn't think Mrs. Fleagle would stoop that low."

"Well, she has, hasn't she?" Earl said.

"I don't suppose this is Paige's handwriting, then?" Larry said.

"Not even close," Earl said. "Hers is very neat and slants forward."

Earl flopped back against the seat in the back. I leaned against the door. Margo turned around in the front seat to face Larry who sat with his head resting on his fist. We were all stumped.

"Is Marilyn Fleagle our woman?" Margo asked, as if it came as a great surprise.

"I don't think so," Larry said.

"What're you talking about?" Earl said. "If she's not, Paige is, and you have absolutely nothing to base that on."

"Think of this, though, Earl. If it was all fabricated—Mrs. Fleagle made up the whole thing, in other words—why the story about someone telling Paige that the girl had been at her apartment building? It's a story we can't substantiate, and it serves only one person: Paige. It makes it appear that the girl really has come around."

"I could see this Fleagle woman's purpose," Earl said. "She could have sent the 'neighbor' to talk to Paige this morning. Perhaps she just said she lived on the next floor. No one would have noticed a woman of such average description."

"It's a long shot," Larry said.

"It is not a long shot," Earl said. "It's the most likely possibility we have."

"All right, Earl, if you want to run with it this way," Larry said, "where do we go from here? How do we determine that it's Marilyn Fleagle who dreamed up this whole thing? What's her point? What's she trying to accomplish?"

"I don't know. That's what we need to find out. What would you suggest?"

"I would suggest that we not put all our eggs in Mrs. Fleagle's basket, and if you argue with me, Earl, you're going to regret it."

"How do you mean?"

"Simply that you are not functioning at full capacity, because you are in love with a woman who could be doing a number on us. I'm not saying she is, mind you. I'm just saying that if it were any other situation and any other case, you would not think twice about simply checking out the stories of *both* women."

"What's there to check out, Larry? Mrs. Fleagle says Paige gave her a note for the young girl, which raises more questions than it answers. It's not Paige's handwriting, she wouldn't be dumb enough to try it anyway, and besides, she has no teen daughter."

"Philip should go to Saint Paul and check her out," Larry said. "And soon. Who knows what this noon tomorrow threat is all about?"

Earl pressed his lips tight and shook his head in resignation. "I said you could handle this thing, Ship, so do whatever you feel is necessary. I suppose you know this is coming out of my pocket. I mean, just exactly who are we representing here?"

"Is money the problem, boss?"

"Of course not. I just think you're barking up the wrong tree."

"Don't worry, Earl," Larry said. "While Philip is in Minnesota, I'll be Marilyn Fleagle's beagle."

"Cute."

"For now," Larry said, "I've got to get Philip to the airport."

"Then I'm heading back to the office," Earl said. "Tell Paige I'll call her tonight and see her in the morning, OK?"

I arrived in St. Paul early that afternoon and started with the phone book. Sure enough, there was a P. Holiday listed at 314 Main Street. I headed to the University. Student records showed that Paige Greene had married a Holiday while a junior, but their records were incomplete after her first job as a nurses' aide in a suburban hospital.

My cab bills mounted as I traveled to the medical center. "Yes," I was told, "Paige Greene was an employee here, and a good one, until she went into teaching special education in the early nineteen seventies." I left for the school board office.

A gentleman in records there said he did not know any of the employees personally, but he did note that a district supervisor had added a comment on Paige

121

Greene Holiday's record. "Would you care to read it yourself?" he asked.

I turned the file folder to face me. "Mrs. Holiday has been an exemplary employee. Our loss is Maplewood's gain. Highest references."

"Maplewood?" I said.

The man reorganized the folder and stepped to the file cabinet. "It's a facility for severely retarded young people. We've lost more than a few teachers to Maplewood."

"But I thought the special education in the public schools had been phased out and reorganized under another state department."

"Pardon me?"

"Not so?"

"No, sir. There have been cutbacks in some areas, but special ed was not one. Of course, teachers can make more money and can often rise faster to higher levels of responsibility when they choose to move to private centers, but no, there has been no phasing out of special ed in our school district."

"I'm sorry. Tell me again when Mrs. Holiday left the employ of the district."

The man didn't even have to check the file again. "At the end of the last term," he said. "Five months ago."

"Maplewood Center for the Mentally Retarded," I told the cabbie, and I began digging through Paige's personnel file once more.

There was no record of Maplewood. She had simply left it out. Either it was a short-term job, or she never really took it. Her records showed that she put her affairs in order, rented her apartment, and packed to move. By the time we pulled into the grounds, the administrator, Mr. Richards, was short of time. "We're closing," he said.

"Just a moment, please," I said. "It's important. I'm a friend of Paige Holiday's, and I just wanted to double-check on her work record here."

The man was taken aback. "How do I know you're a friend of hers?" he said.

"Um, well, what do you want to know? I'll tell you to prove it."

"Where did she work before she came here?" he said, sounding as I had sounded all afternoon.

"School District number seven-oh-nine in special ed," I said.

"And what is her husband's name?"

"I, uh, don't know that, sir, except I know that he died some time back."

"I'm sorry?" Mr. Richards said.

"You didn't know that?"

"Who's asking whom the question here, young man?" he said. "This is highly unusual."

"I know it is, but someone is trying to set up Mrs. Holiday or scare her or something, and I'm a private investigator from Chicago trying to help her."

"Do you have any identification?"

"Sure." I showed him my card.

"You're not a very good special agent for the EH Detective Agency, are you, Mr. Spence?" he said, reading carefully.

"Sir?"

"I say you are not a very good one, are you?"

"That may be, sir, but I don't follow."

"I mean you know very little about the woman you claim to represent. You did say you are representing her, did you not?"

"I'm not sure I said it, but yes, in this instance I am representing her, yes, sir."

"And you say her husband passed away some time ago."

"Not real long ago, as I understand it." I felt stupid. He had somehow put me on the defensive, and I couldn't stay with him.

"Tell me more about Mrs. Holiday," he said. "Convince me that you know her personally."

"I thought you were short of time, sir."

"I've got plenty of time for this. Go on."

"Well, she lives in Chicago and works in a rehabilitation center for autistic children. She worked as a nurses' aide before she taught special ed in the schools here. She went to the University of Minnesota."

"Very interesting."

"But not true?" I said, sheepish for some reason.

"Mostly true. Tell me, Spence, what does she look like?"

I didn't know what in the world Richards was driving at. It wouldn't have surprised me if he had said the woman was his own wife and then produced her from under his desk. He really seemed to enjoy sporting with me.

"Well, ah, she's about forty, and—"

"You know she's forty from her records. What does she look like?"

"Right. She's average height. Built sort of cuddly—" I knew when I said it that he would raise his eyebrows. He did. "Um, she's got pretty dark hair and bright eyes, a beautiful smile."

"Was that pretty hair that's dark or hair that is pretty dark?"

"Honestly, Mr. Richards, must we play this game? Do I have the wrong place or the wrong woman, or are you not really the director here, or what?"

The hint of a smile left his face. "I thought you had been putting *me* on," he said. "Now you say *I've* been playing games. I'll tell you this, I don't consider terribly funny your coming in here and asking a lot of questions about a short-term employee."

"I hadn't intended them to be funny."

"I don't consider it even appropriate."

"I'm sorry. I'm puzzled again."

"The woman's husband is not dead, Mr. Spence. And I guarantee you she is not living in Chicago or working anywhere. She's buried less than a mile from here."

Chapter Fourteen

I must have turned white. I couldn't speak. "Obviously someone is playing a very dirty trick on you, Mr. Spence. How can I help you?"

I was nearly choked up. All I could think of were the ramifications. Was it possible that everything Paige had said was a lie? Why would she want to pose as someone else, and a dead woman at that?

"I think I'd like to talk to her husband," I said. "Would that be possible?"

"I don't know. I'll call him. Would you care to wait in the outer office?"

"Sure. Is there a phone I can use to call my office collect?"

Bonnie answered. She could tell I was shaken. "What's the matter, Philip?"

"I need to talk to Earl right away."

"He just left and took his infrared camera with him."

"Is anyone else around?"

"No, they're all at the rehab center, I think. I was about to leave for home myself. What can I do for you, Philip?"

"Just have someone meet me at O'Hare just after midnight. If I can't make the late flight out of here, I'll get a message to you somehow. Otherwise, be sure someone is there."

Mr. Paul Holiday, located at 314 Main Street, was not excited about my visit, but he was cordial. I asked him to tell me about his wife.

"There's not much to tell. We never had any children, except one that died at birth many years ago. Paige loved children and liked helping people, so she always worked at jobs that served others. I make a good living as a construction engineer, but we really thought our ship had come in when she was offered the job at Maplewood. It was close to home and meant a tremendous increase in salary. I think she always would rather have had children, but short of that, she was fulfilled by helping people and being successful in her career."

"Do you mind my asking how she passed away?"

"She was killed in a car accident."

"I'm sorry."

"I am, too. It really hasn't been that long, you know."

"Mr. Holiday, do you know any *other* Paige Holidays?"

"Nope, not any more."

"Any more?"

"My younger sister's name was Paige. For the first couple of years of our marriage that really caused a lot of confusion. My wife had been Paige Greene and married me to become Paige Holiday, giving us two in the family. Strange, huh?"

128

I heard myself saying, "Yeah, I'd say that's strange," but I don't know how I got it out. "Your, uh, sister, she didn't, ah, happen to marry a guy by the name of Datilo, did she?"

I caught Mr. Holiday in the middle of lighting his cigarette. He stopped and the match burned close to his finger before he shook it out, squinting at me all the while. "Nicholas Datilo," he said. "You got it. Nicky. A bum. He changed her."

"Sir?"

"I don't want to talk about it."

"Where is your sister now?"

"I don't know, and I don't want to know."

"Is she in trouble?"

"It sounds like you know, Mr. Spence. Why don't *you* tell *me*?"

"I just want to be sure I've got the right woman. I embarrassed myself earlier by thinking I was talking about your sister when I was talking about your wife."

"That *would* be embarrassing," Mr. Holiday said. "There's no comparison."

I hoped that by getting him to talk more about his wife, he'd tell me enough about his sister so I would know if we were locking horns with her or with someone using her name and his wife's history.

"No comparison, huh? They don't look at all alike?"

"Not really. I'd have to say my sister is the more striking. Paige, my wife, was never a raving beauty or anything. Pleasant enough looking, but she didn't have my sister's smile. Ah, I don't want to talk about it."

"Your sister's husband changed her?"

"She used to be a great girl. A long time ago, admittedly. But by the time she had her second child, he had changed her."

"Two kids?"

"A girl and a boy. Peggy's about sixteen by now, I'd say. Nobody knows where she is, either. She left about three years ago when little Ronnie died."

"The brother?"

"Yeah. There was a big investigation because my sister and her husband accused each other of having beaten him before he died."

I was in over my head. I could hardly comprehend all this. "So, when did her husband die?"

"Nicky? He didn't die. The kid, the three-year-old, Ronnie, he died."

"Your sister isn't a widow?"

"No. Divorced."

"Could I ask you something, Mr. Holiday? Do you think your sister beat your nephew to death?"

"Yes."

"Sure?"

"Yes."

"Why?"

"Because Peggy told me she saw it happen, and Peggy never lied."

"Were you close to Peggy?"

"Not close enough, I guess."

"Ever hear from her?"

"Now and then. We never know where from, really.

The postmarks follow her around the country. She called me one night and asked if her mother had left town. I told her I would try to find out. When the phone had been disconnected and the mail returned unforwardable, I knew her mother was gone."

"You don't know where she is?"

"No. And like I say, I don't care to know, except that Peggy wants to find her."

"Do you know why?"

"I'm afraid to think why."

"Sir?"

"She once said she wanted to kill her, but she was waiting for her to get out of the Twin Cities so it wouldn't be so obvious."

"I need to get back to Chicago," I said. "I sure appreciate the time you've taken and how forthright you've been with me."

"Quite all right. Depressing, isn't it? You never did tell me why you wanted all this information."

"We may have found your sister in the Chicago area."

"Well, you can have her. I just hope you don't find my niece there, too."

Chapter Fifteen

Mr. Holiday rummaged around and came up with old photographs of both his sister, Paige Holiday Datilo, and his niece, Peggy. I assured him I would mail them back as soon as possible. It was eerie to stare into the beautiful smile of Earl's love and to know that she was not at all what he thought she was.

With the way this case had been going, I knew I should double-check her brother's story. Who knew what reason this man might have for discrediting his own sister?

The cab had been waiting, the meter clicking, and the cabbie reading the *Twin Cities Telegraph*. He looked up and smiled when I opened the door. "Any more stops, pal?"

"I've got a problem," I said. "I need to get to the office of the paper you're reading, and then I need to get to the airport for an eleven o'clock flight."

"Start the countdown, commander," he said, grinning in the rearview mirror and racing off.

We arrived at the newspaper office with only a few minutes to spare before their public information center closed. "Please let me check something on microfilm real quick," I begged the girl.

"Do you know exactly what you're looking for, or are you going to have to check through a bunch of films?"

"Just give me June, three years ago, and I'll be outa here in fifteen minutes."

She popped open a box and threaded the machine in seconds. Deftly whipping the crank, she rolled to the front page, June 1. "There you go," she said. "I want to leave here at ten after."

"You got it," I said, and I started cranking. When the June 9 pages rolled into view, the headline appeared in the lower left-hand corner of the third page:

MOTHER ACCUSED OF CHILD
MURDER STANDS TRIAL TODAY

The article told the story of the tragic death of three-year-old Ronnie Datilo and the finger-pointing by both parents. One paragraph reported the police opinion that the thirteen-year-old daughter might have been a witness, but that she had been scared out of testifying and was in seclusion.

I cranked through the folowing days' coverage of the trial and came upon a photo of an unsmiling Paige with a bandana covering her hair, her collar turned up, and her eyes hidden by sunglasses. She was acquitted because she had successfully turned enough attention onto her estranged husband. The opinion of many jurors was that he had committed the crime, but that "even if she did it, he should share the blame."

There was great public outcry, and Mrs. Datilo left for parts unknown. Her husband never stood trial, though the papers reported that the daughter was believed to be staying with him. According to Paul Holiday, Paige Datilo's brother, she didn't stay there long. She had been chasing her mother all over the country.

And now she had found her. I ran for the cab.

"You've got plenty of time now," the cabbie said. "You could get out of the Twin Cities by nine."

"That's what I want to do," I said.

I landed at O'Hare Field at a few minutes after ten and ran through the terminal to the rental car desk. I was huffing and puffing as I asked for whatever car was available and slapped my credit card on the counter. "O.J. Simpson you're not," the girl joked. I couldn't even smile.

On my way out to the car, I phoned Bonnie's home. "Tell whoever was going to pick me up that they don't have to now."

"I was going to pick you up," she said, "so this *is* good news. Did you turn up anything there?"

"I really don't have time to go into it, Bon. I'm sorry. I gotta go."

"I understand, Philip. Are you aware that the girl showed up again?"

I had nearly hung up the phone. "What?"

"Peggy Datilo showed up at the rehab center asking for Paige after hours. Mrs. Fleagle was not in, but the receptionist phoned her at home and let Peggy talk to her. Peggy told Mrs. Fleagle where Paige was to meet her tonight."

"Tonight? Peggy's meeting Paige tonight?"

135

"That's what she wants."

"Do you know where they're supposed to meet?"

"No, but Larry and Earl and Margo do. They're on their way to Paige's apartment now."

"If you hear from anyone, Bonnie, tell 'em I'm on my way there too. And tell 'em not to do anything until I get there, including allowing Paige to meet with Peggy."

I was lucky to avoid a speeding ticket on my way to Paige's apartment building near the rehab center. I pulled into the parking lot where Margo, Larry, and Earl were just getting into Larry's car. I flashed my lights and wheeled close to them before realizing that they would not recognize the car. I saw Earl reach inside his coat just in case.

"It's me," I said, rolling down the window.

"Let's talk in my car," Shipman said, and we all climbed in.

"Bonnie told me that Peggy is demanding a meeting," I said.

"That's not all," Larry said, "Mrs. Fleagle claims she told Paige that Peggy wanted to meet her in the unlit northwest corner of the municipal park in Mount Prospect about an hour from now, and warned her not to bring anyone with her. Earl called Paige to see what she was going to do, and she claimed that Mrs. Fleagle had never told her any such thing and that she wouldn't sit still for any meeting anyway, especially with some crazy girl claiming to be her long lost daughter."

"I think we've got Mrs. Fleagle dead to rights," Earl said. "But I still don't know what she's trying to pull."

"But the girl exists," Larry said. "The receptionist told us she saw Peggy."

"She could have been saying what her boss told her to say," Earl said.

"No, she wasn't," Margo said. "That woman was not lying."

"You can't know that," Earl said.

"We can find out," I said, producing the old photograph of the girl. "Let's show this to the receptionist. I think I've found Peggy Datilo."

"What's *this* all about?" Earl said.

"I'm not sure yet," I said. "Let's check and see if the woman at the receptionist desk identifies her. Meanwhile, you can tell me what you're doing here."

Larry started the car. "Paige told Earl she wanted to be alone tonight and asked him not to come over," he said. "Margo got suspicious and wondered if maybe Mrs. Fleagle was telling the truth and really *had* told Paige about Peggy's demands. When Earl called Paige to double-check, there was no answer. We got no response at her door, and her car is gone."

"Do you think she'll try to meet Peggy?"

"If there *is* a Peggy," Earl said, still dubious.

Larry stopped near the front door of the rehab center, and we all trotted in. "That's her," the receptionist said, studying the picture. "She's older, but this is the girl."

"All right," Earl said. "The girl is for real. And maybe Mrs. Fleagle has been telling the truth all along. Philip, I've gotta know what you found out."

I told the story fast as Larry sped back to Paige's

137

building. Earl stayed in the car with his head in his hands while the other three of us ran to the elevator.

"We really need to know where she is," Larry explained as he whacked loudly on the door. No answer. "Help me, Philip," he said, and we lowered our shoulders into the door.

It creaked and cracked, but it was heavy and wouldn't give. Larry motioned me out of the way and drove his foot into the right side, just under the knob. The door blew open, ripping the inside frame molding with it. We flipped the lights on. The apartment was empty. No clothes in the closets, no pictures on the walls, nothing but furniture and a little trash.

"Now," Margo said, "is she going to see Peggy, or has she simply left?"

"I don't know," Larry said, "but we can't take any chances after what Philip says she told her uncle."

We waited as long as we could for the elevator, then bounded down the stairs. Earl was not in Larry's car, and Earl's car was gone. "This is all we need," Margo said.

"It's time to go to Mount Prospect," Shipman said.

Larry turned off his lights as we neared the park and rolled to the curb about a block and a half away. "Is that Paige's car down there?" Margo asked.

"It's hard to tell," Larry said, "but if that other one is Earl's—and I think it is—he can see it more clearly. I don't know what he thinks he's going to do."

"Maybe shoot pictures with his infrared camera?" I guessed.

"No way," Margo said. "He left it right here on the floor." She pulled it up to show us.

"Let me see that," Larry said. "A few well-placed shots will at least prove Paige was here, in case she tries to deny it later."

"Why would she do that?"

"Who knows why she does anything?" Larry said. "I can't figure the woman. How does she maintain this incredible facade?"

"That's me too," Margo agreed. "It's hard to believe."

"I just thought of something, Larry," I said. "Are you carrying a gun?"

"You know I'm not licensed yet."

"I know. But are you carrying one anyway?"

"No, Earl finally made me give him all of mine so he wouldn't get in trouble if I got caught with one."

"Great."

"Why?"

"Because the only one of the four of us with a gun is Earl. And Peggy did—at one time at least—intend to kill her mother."

"Earl knows that, and I don't think he'll let Paige get out of her car if Peggy shows."

"But Earl is more concerned with his relationship with her than with this meeting," Margo said. "Isn't he going to want to know how she could have lied to him so much? Won't that be the first thing on his mind?"

"You may be right," Shipman said, tinkering with the camera and thinking. "Paige doesn't want to see him again, I think."

"How do you know?" I said.

"Because she's packed for the road. She probably figures a short meeting with Peggy will be easier than a confrontation with Earl. I think she's getting ready to totally stiff him. He'll never hear from her again."

"But Larry," Margo said, "there are a few things working against Paige right now, and Earl is the least of them. She doesn't know her daughter wants to kill her—"

"Don't be too sure about that," Larry interrupted. "She's not stupid. The girl has had a horrible life and was surely traumatized by what she saw. In fact, she was probably an abused child herself."

"OK, but still, I doubt Paige knows that Peggy has actually said she wanted to kill her mother. Anyway, regardless of what Paige feels or doesn't feel for Peggy, she *is* her daughter, and Paige has to be curious. I'm betting that Paige wants to get a look at her, even if she's afraid to actually talk to her."

"You don't think Paige is concerned with Earl now?" I asked.

"Not really," Margo said. "She has to know that what she's done to him can never be justified or reconciled. She's gonna just leave him in the dust. She may communicate shame or sorrow to him someday, somehow, but for now, she's leaving him behind."

Shipman appeared to have the camera figured out. "What do you think, Philip," he said. "Is there anything to what Margo's saying?"

"She knows the female mind," I said. "In fact, she

often knows the male mind, too. I wouldn't bet against her."

"So what's Earl going to do, Margo?" Larry asked.

"I already told you. He knows the story, knows Peggy is more than a figment of someone's imagination, and knows that Paige has been phony. He just wants to know how she could have done it. I say he'll be ignoring Peggy and concentrating on Paige."

"So why doesn't he approach Paige's car?"

"I don't know. Are we even sure those cars belong to who we think they do? And if they do, and we've got the right place, where's Peggy?"

"Right there," Larry said in a whisper, pointing down the street at a slim, young girl walking resolutely into the park. She passed under a street light and into the shadows where she stopped and leaned back against a huge tree.

And waited.

Chapter Sixteen

"Keep your eyes on Paige's car, Margo," Larry said. "She probably doesn't know how to get out without letting the inside light come on. If you see that light, let me know. Philip, you watch Earl's car, though you probably won't see anything, even if he gets out.

"I'm counting on your amateur psychology, Margo," Larry continued. "When Paige realizes she can't get a good look at her daughter from where she is, I say she'll venture out."

"And that's when Earl will make his move?" I said.

"Earl is going to be hard to figure tonight, Philip. If I were Earl, I would want to get to Paige before she gets to her daughter, knowing what we know. Maybe he's just here to see if she lied to him about coming, and once he's sure it's her, he'll leave."

"You think he'll leave when he sees Paige get out of her car?" Margo asked, incredulous.

"Right."

"Wrong," she said. "No way he's gonna drive off and leave her to her daughter, no matter what she's done to him."

"But he knows we're here to protect Paige," Ship countered.

"He also knows you're not carrying a gun," Margo said. "What're you gonna do, shoot it out with a camera?"

Larry shrugged.

"Here we sit," Margo said. "C'mon, we've got to do something."

"Let me think," Larry said. "But keep watching those cars. Do either of you have a long comb?"

"I do," Margo said, digging it out of her purse without taking her eyes off Paige's car. "What do you need it for?"

"You'll see." Larry opened his door a crack and pressed the comb against the button that keeps the light off when the door is closed. "If I can jam it in here right," he said, "we can all get out without worrying about the light coming on and giving us away."

"All of us?" Margo said. "What am I supposed to do?"

"I want us to beat everyone to the punch," Larry said. "Earl may be already out and in the park, but we just don't know. I think I can walk around the block and come in the park from behind where Peggy is. If I can pull it off, I'll be behind that big stone hearth over there about twenty feet to her left and behind her about ten feet. See it?"

Margo and I stole a peek from our car vigils. "Yeah," we said.

"Philip," Larry said slowly, "I have a real chore for you."

144

"You do, huh?"

"Are you up to it?"

"Depends."

"No, it doesn't depend. In many ways we have to be like the military. Either you're ready to do exactly as you're told, or your job is in jeopardy. You realize I'm in charge of this."

"Of course, Larry. I was only kidding."

"This isn't the time to kid. I want you to get to the other side of the tree Peggy is leaning against. You'll have to be quieter than you've ever been in your life, and you'd better take some kind of a weapon in case she's armed. Which she very well could be."

"How do I get there without her noticing?"

"You go the major part of the way with me, then veer off to the right behind the trees. It's important you get to her tree because you may have to keep her from harming Paige."

"I have no weapon."

"I have two substitutes in my glove compartment. Take your pick while I watch Earl's car."

I dug around in the glove box and came up with a folded wire hanger Shipman used when he locked himself out of his car, and a huge flashlight. "I'll take this," I said.

"Just make sure it doesn't go on," Shipman said. "It'll light up the whole place. Margo, I want you to walk down the other side of the street. There are no lights between here and Earl's car, so you won't be seen. If you happen to get there before he gets out, I want you to do whatever you have to do to keep him right where he is. He's going to be good for nothing here tonight, so if there's a way to keep him in that car or at least out of the park, do it. OK?"

"OK."

"What'll you be doing, Ship?"

"Taking pictures. Say, 'Cheese.' Let's go."

The three of us made it out of the car without incident, though Margo had to climb over the back of the front seat to get out Larry's jimmied door. "I would take your assignment, Philip," he explained before Margo left, "but I'm a lot bigger than you are, and I don't think I could get close to her without her hearing me."

I knew it was true, because I knew Ship was fearless and usually demanded the most dangerous assignment. He'd be close enough if there was trouble.

We could see Margo moving slowly up the far side of the street, a long block from Earl's car. "Don't walk on either heel or toe once we get into the park," Larry whispered. "You want your foot to hit flat, distributing the weight and deadening noise." He demonstrated in the gravel at the side of the road as we crossed the street to enter the far side of the park. It was as if he were walking in stocking feet on carpet.

"What if Paige drives off?" I asked.

"We watch to see what Earl does. If he goes after her, we go after him. Let Peggy fend for herself; she seems to have done all right up to now. I just want to be around for Earl's confrontation with Paige. I don't think he'd do anything rash, but I want to protect his pride, too. It

146

would be sad if he made a fool of himself."

"He probably thinks he already has," I said.

We were about 150 feet from Larry's station. He put out a hand to stop me. "No more talk," he whispered. "I'll just signal you."

We crept up behind the hearth, running our fingers along the huge rocks and cement that made up its back side. Larry was just ahead of me and motioned that I should follow him. When he got to the edge of the far side he stopped and bent low, peeking around the corner. He grabbed my shirt and pulled my ear close to his mouth. "I have a perfect view of her," he whispered. "You go back around the other way and take your time getting to the tree. Silence is the priority, not speed. If anything happens before you get there, I'll handle it."

By the time I had sneaked around the other side of the stone hearth I could see Peggy's silhouette between me and a distant streetlight. I wasn't thirty feet from her, yet I was convinced she could hear my heart crashing against my ribs. I took a step, cracked a twig, and stopped dead. She hadn't heard. She didn't move. Neither did I.

I waited. When my breath came a little more evenly, I ventured forward again. I was trying to walk so quietly I could hardly keep my balance. I could barely see the metal of the flashlight in my left hand. *What in the world am I gonna do with this?* I wondered. I looked past Peggy to the street. I couldn't see either car, though I knew if either Earl or Paige got out without fixing the light button, I'd see.

By now, Margo had to be at Earl's car, and for that I was grateful. I was convinced she could keep him away long enough for us to find out if Peggy was really going to try anything.

When I was twenty feet behind Peggy, any possible view of me was hidden by the tree she leaned against. I stopped to catch my breath and relax a little. The stretch where she could have spotted me had seemed like a hundred miles, though it wasn't really more than forty feet. Now I had to get up behind her. She wouldn't see me unless she heard me and came around the tree to look, so I had to be slower and quieter than ever.

There were big trees between us, so if she did come, I could hide momentarily. Maybe it would give me time to either blind her with the flashlight or yell so Ship could help me, but we'd really have to get the drop on her to elude a weapon of any force. I couldn't imagine a sixteen- or seventeen-year-old girl carrying a gun, but this was no ordinary girl. Who knew where she had been living, or with whom, for the past three years? And what must it have taken for her to track down her mother, who was using her maiden name and her sister-in-law's history?

I was ten feet from the big tree. It was so immense that I couldn't see her. I knew she was still there because otherwise I would have heard her leave. My eyes had long since adjusted to the darkness, and I was amazed at what I could see in what had at first appeared pitch black. I would have to avoid a small branch on the ground, and I was glad the leaves in the area were still moist. There was no way I could have moved undetected through crisp dry leaves. As it was I felt like an elephant in baseball cleats trying to tiptoe through peanut brittle.

I had to open my mouth to keep from making too much noise breathing. It seemed as if I were gasping, my chest heaving. Surely she could hear me. But she didn't. Or at least there was no indication that she did.

Now there was nothing between me and the big tree. Nowhere to hide, nowhere to run. I had to make it and press myself up against it. By now I should have been in Larry's line of sight, and for some strange reason I wanted to appear brave and self-confident, should he be watching. I took a slow and, I hoped, quiet, deep breath, straightened up, and began moving, one torturous step at a time. The last three steps were excruciatingly slow and painful because the tension had caused cramps in my legs and even in my back.

I couldn't imagine that she didn't hear me, because I could hear her. Every time her weight shifted or she sighed, it was as if she were standing right next to me. Which, of course, except for several tons of tree trunk, she was. I laid my cheek up against the cool bark and smelled deep of the wood. I could see the shadowy outline of Larry's form crouching twenty feet back and ten feet over at the end of the hearth.

Somehow, his being there lent very little comfort. I was not five feet from a girl who might be intent on killing someone tonight, and if I got in her way I could be the victim. What could he do? I wondered if he was already taking pictures and what in the name of Sherlock

Holmes he thought he was going to do with them.

I couldn't relax or slow my heart rate or breathing. Any sound or sensed movement from the other side made me flinch, and I was certain she knew I was there. I didn't dare peek around to see if anyone was coming because it would have brought me too close to her line of sight.

I watched Larry for several minutes, trying to take my mind off my predicament, anything to make the time move faster. Where was this going to lead? At one point I thought I saw him raise a fist and then duck back behind the hearth wall, as if to encourage me to hang in there.

Finally, I heard footsteps from in front of the tree. I wanted to look, but I knew I would be seen. I stayed still. The steps stopped about ten feet in front of Peggy. I heard Peggy move forward a foot or so, but neither person said anything for several seconds. Peggy spoke first.

"I'm glad you came, Mother. I wasn't sure you would."

"I've been here quite a while, actually," Paige said, still sounding sweet, though a little subdued. "I just wanted to watch you for a while from the street."

"I don't hate you anymore, you know," Peggy said.

"No, I didn't know."

"I might have killed you if I had found you six months ago. But I started living with a guy who slapped me around a lot, the way Daddy used to do to you. It made me crazy. It made me want to kill my guy and my dad, but it changed how I felt about you a little."

150

Paige did not respond. The girl sounded so calm, as if she had carefully planned what she was going to say. She waited and then spoke again. "I still hate what you do, passing yourself off as someone else, refusing to try to get in touch with me. I know you don't love me, but you can quit worrying that I'll come forward and tell what you used to do to me and what you did to Ronnie."

"I may never quit worrying about that, Peggy," Paige said. "You were always a rebel, always a conniver, always saying whatever you had to to get your own way. Why should I trust you now? You know where I am; you know my alias. I don't remember loving you since you were a baby, so what do you want from me?"

I could hardly believe what I was hearing. There must have been a lot about this strange relationship that I didn't know. The daughter tries to make up with the murdering, abusing, and abused mother, yet the mother suspects her.

"I want nothing from you. I just wanted you to know that my search is over. I'm not forgiving you for anything, and I'm not even sure that keeping silent is the right thing to do, since you did kill Ronnie. Regardless of the pressures you were under, you didn't have to beat him. But you *were* under pressure, and now I know that. That's all I wanted you to know, and I'm satisfied to be through with you. You've been through with me for longer than I can remember."

"Why don't I trust you even now?" Paige whined, as if she really wanted to.

"I don't trust you either, Mother, so don't worry about it."

151

"I *am* worried about it. And I *don't* trust you. And that's why I must make sure you don't tell what you saw."

"I just told you not to worry about it."

"And I told you I didn't trust you."

Paige fumbled in her purse, and it dropped to the ground. Peggy spun around to my side of the tree, bumped into me, and screamed.

Chapter Seventeen

I flipped on the flashlight and twisted around to the other side just as Paige flew forward, a gun in her hand. I dropped in front of her and heard the shot as she tumbled over me, flashlight and gun flying in different directions.

I grabbed her around the waist and pinned her to the ground as Larry gathered up the gun and flashlight. Earl ran past at full tilt after Peggy, with Margo not far behind.

"I can't stop him!" Margo cried. "He thinks Peggy shot her mother!"

Larry took off after them, shouting and waving the flashlight. "When I arrived," he said later, "Peggy was on the ground, staring into Earl's revolver and pleading for her life."

Peggy was not held after she was questioned at the police station. Paige was booked on attempted murder but refused to talk to Earl or let him try to bail her out. He was exhausted.

The day had begun to get to me, too. I had been up early, thinking I was going to get to tell my friends and co-workers about my faith, and since then I had been in another state, had run around in a park, and nearly got my head blown off.

Margo sat close and put her arm around me. "Earl needs us," she said quietly. We sat in a spare interrogation room and asked Earl if he wanted to talk.

"I don't know," he said, his voice thick. "You know

if she hadn't pulled this tonight, she could have been home free. Now she may never be free again."

There was nothing to say. On all of our minds was her performance over the past several days, living someone else's life with someone else's name, and winning our hearts. Especially Earl's.

"I don't know what I would have thought of her if she hadn't done this tonight," he said.

Shipman stared him full in the face.

"I think maybe I would have been able to forgive her, to see her side of it, to understand why she had to hide from herself and her past. But now. She had no compassion, no honesty. Hardly anything that came from her mouth has been truth ever since I've known her. I just wonder what she thought of me."

"Do you really want to know?" Ship asked.

"Probably not. Maybe she's trying to tell me right now. I did love her, there's no getting around it. She was, or seemed, a wonderful, loving person."

He was fighting tears. "We all need sleep," Margo said.

"I won't be sleeping tonight," he said, sounding old. "What do you make of this, Margo?"

"Pardon?"

"What do you make of the fact that I seem to get one break, one chance at love after all these years, and it not only goes up in smoke, but it nearly consumes me in the process."

"I don't know, Earl," she said. "I just know that we all love you and care about you, and we're feeling terrible for you."

He nodded without looking at her. Shipman stood and clapped Earl on the shoulder, letting his hand linger.

"What'd you get in the way of pictures tonight, Lar?" Earl said.

"Aw, nothing really."

"C'mon! I know you were shooting. What'd you get?"

"Well, I got several shots of Peggy waiting at the tree, and a few of Philip behind her. And, frankly, I think I got a shot of Paige and Philip just before she fell over him."

"In other words," Earl said sadly, "you have a picture of Paige trying to shoot her own daughter."

Shipman dropped his head and nodded. "You asked," he said.

"That's my camera, right?" Earl said.

"Yeah."

"And that was my film, too, right?"

"Yeah."

"May I have it, please?"

Larry handed it to him. Earl carefully took the camera from its case and popped the back off. He pulled the film from its cannister and dropped it into the waste basket. He rose wearily and pulled his coat on.

"Take a day off tomorrow, kids," he said. "I'm going to."

We trudged out to Larry's car and rode in silence to the street next to the park where Earl had left his car. "You gonna be all right, chief?" Larry asked as Earl got out.

"Yeah. I'll see you Wednesday. Philip, walk me to my car."

I got out quickly, puzzled. Earl didn't say anything.

"I want you to know that what Margo said goes for all of us, Earl. No matter how hot we might have gotten at you during the course of all this—"

"I know," he said. "Philip, I just don't know how to explain all this, and I don't want you to even pretend to try. But I do want you to talk to the staff Wednesday morning like you were going to today. Grief, it seems like a week ago.

"Anyway, take all the time you need. No restrictions. And I'm not telling you I'm about to buy any of it; in fact, I probably never will. But I think I know a little of how you felt when this Dahlberg boy died. If you've got something you want to say, I want you to say it."

He stuck out his hand. I couldn't remember when I had last shaken hands with Earl. I gripped it hard. "See you Wednesday morning," I said.

"Bright and early," he said.

"Bright and early."

In Margo Mystery No. 5, *Allyson,* Philip is assigned the biggest investigation of his career. The beautiful Allyson is in search of her father's history, a history that seems to have vanished. The case takes Philip to Israel and jeopardizes his love for Margo.